TIN
SOLDIERS

The Story of Los Niños Héroes

E. Richard Amiel

Tin Soldiers by E. Richard Amiel
© 2015 E Richard Amiel

ISBN: 0692465995
ISBN 13: 9780692465998
Library of Congress Control Number: 2015943465
Dead Bird, Whittier, CA

I would like to thank Guru Nam Singh (my uncle Lalo), who believed in me and encouraged me to make my dream of writing my first book a reality.

I would also like to give a special thank-you to my mother. Not only did she give me life, but she also taught me how to live it. No, seriously, she tells me how to live my life. I love you, Mom. Thank you for literally everything good in my life.

I also thank my *abuelita* Lupe Diaz Portillo (Nana), whom I miss terribly. How I truly wish you were here to read my first book. I will always love you.

Finally, this book is for the Mexican people, whose country is full of rich history, breathtaking landscapes, and the most genuine people I know. Their people continue to have a resounding echo that was heard in 1810 and is still relevant today—freedom!

AUTHOR'S NOTE

There will be many times in our lives when we will make decisions without truly knowing the outcome. Some of these decisions may come with disastrous results. We attempt to rationalize them, convincing ourselves that we made them with the best intentions. But what may appear correct may not be the same as what is right. We then reflect and ask ourselves, did we make the decision out of instinct, or did we make it to better a nation? And that can lead to drastic decisions that result in tragic consequences to one side or the other. We try to pinpoint where or when the decision was made and where it started to go wrong. Once we come to that point, we simply accept it as a mistake and never look back. Nonetheless, if we continue to make the same thoughtless decisions, we will make the same mistakes. So we have to ask ourselves whether the decisions we make now are just?

If these situations happen to people every day, you can only imagine the decisions made for a whole nation. Those with the highest authority continually make these decisions every day, affecting not only their own lives but also the lives of millions. Decisions arise from vast situations in a moment's time. Decisions must be made in the best interest of the people they are sworn to protect. This has to be the mind-set before one can make a judgment for the future of a young nation.

The outcomes of these decisions will not only change the course of a young nation but also the destiny of two. These decisions will affect two nations and make their mark on history.

History will mark these events as one of the most romantic, patriotic, and dramatic episodes between the United States of America and Mexico.

Tin Soldiers

INTRODUCTION

I. The Difficult Birth of a United and Independent Mexico, 1821–1845

During the first years of the nineteenth century, Spain engaged in a war against France. Napoleon I invaded Spain and placed his brother on the Spanish throne. This affected not only Europe but also Spain's colonies in North America and in Mexico. Spain could not oversee Mexico as it would have wanted, and the Mexican people refused to accept any authority other than Fernando VII, king of Spain. Mexico saw its chance, as did the rest of the Spanish colonies in America, for freedom from Spain's grasp once and for all.

Miguel Hidalgo, a Catholic priest, declared Mexico's independence from Spain on September 16, 1810. The result was a long and costly war in Mexico. Hidalgo was eventually captured and executed by a firing squad on June 26, 1811. The war for independence lasted eleven years and ended with the Treaty of Cordova, which was signed on August 24, 1821.

During its first years of independent life, Mexico faced many obstacles to obtaining unity within. Agustin de Iturbide was a former Spanish general who switched sides and fought for Mexico's independence. He made himself emperor of Mexico. Mexico still felt it lacked any real leadership. Eventually, a revolt broke out, forcing Iturbide to step down as emperor. In 1823, Guadalupe Victoria became the first president of Mexico, which was called the United Mexican States.

The second president, General Manuel Gonzalez, won the electoral vote in 1828. The Conservative Party, under the command of General Anastasio Bustamante, began another revolution, and Bustamante became president of Mexico in 1830. Then, in 1832, the Federalists enlisted General Antonio Lopez de Santa Anna to overthrow Bustamante and install Gomez Pedraza as the true president.

When in office, Pedraza had Congress come together and declare Santa Anna president and Valentin Gomez Farias as vice president. Santa Anna was president in name only, for his interest in the presidency was less to be desired as he believe that true power was to control everything from behind the scenes, and he left Gomez Farias with all the executive duties. Santa Anna returned to his residence in Veracruz. With his newfound power, Gomez Farias tried to make a difference by attempting to eliminate corruption and prevent any more uprisings. He targeted all who had strong ties with Santa Anna and those who had sided with the corrupt: the military, the wealthy landowners, and the clergy.

Once word reached Santa Anna, he immediately returned to Mexico, and Farias relinquished his duties. Santa Anna also disbanded Congress and rewrote the constitution. This infuriated many citizens from different parts of the country and caused many states to rebel against Santa Anna, including Coahuila, Durango, Guanajuato, Jalisco, Michoacán, Queretaro, San Luis Potosi, Texas, Yucatan, and Zacatecas. These states wanted to be independent from Santa Anna's rule. Yet after much debating and negotiating, many of the states just returned to the Mexican government.

When Texas became a republic in 1836, Santa Anna was captured and sent back to his home state in Veracruz. In an effort to redeem himself, he fought against France in the Pastry War of 1838. Once he regained power, Santa Anna was more militant than ever. He became more of a dictator than a liberator, and, little by little, more Mexican states revolted against this self-proclaimed dictatorship. Congress convened and voted General Herrera as a new temporary president to overthrow Santa Anna. Santa Anna would later be imprisoned and exiled to Cuba in 1845.

II. The Republic of Texas and the Strengthening of the United States

To populate Mexico's northern territories, the Mexican government needed to find immigrant families. To achieve this, Mexico looked to its neighbor in the north, the United States. The Mexican government gave land grants to thousands of immigrant families with the intention that these families would convert to Catholicism and eventually become Mexican citizens themselves.

There were many conditions to these land grants. One was that new citizens were not allowed to import slaves. These conditions, like many others, were ignored. The Mexican government could not enforce the conditions because of the distance between the northern territories and the capital of the country. There was great instability within the government itself in Mexico City.

When Santa Anna disbanded Congress and rewrote the constitution, Texas challenged it. Texas wanted its own independence and wanted nothing to do with Mexico or Santa Anna. This uprising was led by the English-speaking immigrant families who settled in Texas. The Republic of Texas was born in 1836. After the siege of the Alamo, Texas eventually gained its independence.

In 1845, the United States annexed Texas. This propelled the United States to begin its course of Manifest Destiny, the idea that America had the right to conquer as much land as it wanted. This included land that still belonged to Mexico. The line had been drawn. Many battles took place, but the last and most remembered battle redefined Mexico as well as the United States. The battle would not only test the bravery of men but also make men out of children. This is their story.

PROLOGUE

Honoring the Past

On a clear, early morning on the empty streets in Mexico City in 1947, a few merchants had begun their day. There were few cars parked on the road. As the sun rose over the mountains, filling the streets with light, the merchants continued to march up and down the road like ants. The streets began to fill with people going about their business. A long, majestic road was located behind a huge forest, leading to a memorial. Locals passed by the memorial not knowing that this would be a very special day.

From a distance, a long black Lincoln surrounded by a motorcade patrolled down the streets of Mexico City. Seated in the back of the Lincoln was a well-dressed gentleman who was admiring the view.

There were other men in the vehicle who seemed to be talking to the gentleman. Their lips moved, but no sound was coming out. The gentleman's eyes were transfixed by the simple beauty of the foreign city that stood before him. The gentleman appeared to be calculating his next step, as though he were about to make a critical chess move. The vehicle arrived at its destination and stopped. Sound began to come out of the men's lips, as if someone had raised the volume of a radio.

"Sir, are you sure about this?" said one of the men.

"It is something that has been long overdue," the distinguished gentleman replied sternly. Then he added, "Let's get on with it."

The car door opened, and his footsteps were the only sound heard. As he came to the end of the walk, he looked straight ahead while holding a floral wreath. The distinguished gentleman had clean-cut gray hair. He was wearing round-rimmed glasses and a very nice suit. Surrounded by bodyguards, he stood in front of a stone monument bearing the name Los Niños Heroes. His presence caused a commotion; people began to fill the monument. Farther back, a sea of people poured into the streets that surrounded the monument.

The monument sat at the basin of the beautiful forest called Chapultepec. There were so many trees and rocks behind the monument that it created another world; its beauty linked to the city. What stood out the most was the Castle of Chapultepec, seemingly pushed up high in the middle of the forest by the hands of the gods. There was much wear and tear all over the great stonewalls. There were many great rooms, and some were used as classrooms. The outside grounds were maintained. Early in the morning, the castle had a tranquil feeling despite being so empty. The castle was more like a museum than the prestigious military school that it had once been.

1

Suddenly, ghostly images of young cadets appeared, walking around the grounds and through the castle. The cadets of years past could now be heard running through the hallways. The date was July 24, 1845.

Two cadets in particular were running through the hallways as if on fire.

"Juan—sorry, I mean Bara—come on, we're going to be so late," said Fernando, catching his breath.

"Well then, wait for me. I left my assignment in the dorm room," Bara replied with little breath of his own.

"If you're late one more time, you're going to be stuck cleaning the stables again!"

"A little horse manure never hurt anyone, Fernando."

"Tell that to my nose."

Bara just laughed as they arrived at their destination. The boys slowly tried to enter their classroom unnoticed, for their class had already been in session ten minutes. They noticed the other students working in silence as the professor wrote an assignment on the chalkboard. The two boys tried to sneak to their seats. Unfortunately for them, he was fully aware.

"So nice of both of you to be joining us this fine morning," Professor Tomas said sternly.

"Sorry, Professor, it's just that—"

"Please, Mr. Barrera, not another one of your many excuses," the professor said, dismayed.

"But Professor, I made up a real good one this time," muttered Bara.

Their classmates began to snicker and laugh softly.

"You would be cleaning the stables if it weren't for your father," Professor Tomas said.

All of a sudden, Juan's smile disappeared, and his face changed into an emotionless state.

"Sir, the simple fact that you use my father as the reason not to punish me"—Bara paused to restrain himself—"entices me to choose to clean the stables, if you so wish."

Once Bara said this, Fernando groaned, for he knew what was coming next.

"Very well. Since it is your choice, you will clean the stables," Professor Tomas replied with annoyance. "And Mr. De Oca will join you as well. But first, report to the director."

Fernando, desperate for an appeal, replied, "But sir, you haven't heard my excuse."

The classroom burst into laughter.

2

During the early morning, the mists began to lift across the eastern countryside of the United States, and the rays of the rising sun lit up the White House. The grass was still wet with dew as two guards stood in front protecting the entrance. In one of the main rooms were three men sitting in lush single chairs. The men were President James T. Polk, Vice President George Dallas, and General Zachary Taylor.

One of the four main campaign issues President Polk had was the westward expansion, which would be referred as Manifest Destiny. Polk believed Manifest Destiny would help shape America as one of the greatest nations in the world. Vice President George Dallas sat attentively while the president and General Taylor talked. The president was a well-groomed man. General Zachary Taylor, on the other hand, did not dress to impress but like a soldier who had been in the field for weeks. His style of dress was wrinkled clothes and a straw hat. General Taylor was a man rough around the edges, and he took pride in being so. General Taylor had seen and been in many wars, so the wear and tear was very visible on his face.

President Polk addressed General Taylor. "Many things have happened to our great nation in the last ten years. For one, Texas gained its independence, and we gained a great state. Now, if you remember, one of my campaign promises was to continue to expand our western borders and eventually extend all the way to California and acquire the Oregon Territory."

"I do believe you fueled a lot of hostilities for such an aggressive expansion, mainly among Mexicans and Americans who still live on that land. Many critics say that this expansion could lead us into war with Britain and Mexico," Taylor said convincingly.

"Critics," Polk interrupted. "These must be the same critics who said I was a dark horse to win the presidency."

General Taylor looked at Dallas to see if a response was needed.

"Besides, the issue with Britain has been resolved, General," Polk said smugly.

"Beg your pardon, Mr. President. I was not aware."

"We have come to a compromise. The boundary will be on the forty-ninth parallel. We still need to sign the treaty, but it is all said and done," Polk continued.

"Well, that's wonderful news, sir," Taylor responded happily.

Polk interrupted again. "It is Mexico I am concerned with, General. I have nothing but contempt for that country and its people. Now it seems we have a situation in lower Texas. The Mexican government is disputing the borderlines between us and them. Nevertheless, you know it is your sworn oath and duty to protect the United States."

"My duty will always be to the United States, Mr. President," Taylor said with much conviction.

"Indeed, sir, but our duty now is to continue to make this nation even greater—a dream that many are calling Manifest Destiny, and I intend to make it true."

Vice President Dallas added, "General, a large majority of Americans support the president's vision for a great continental nation."

Polk continued, "Do you believe in Manifest Destiny, General?"

"That we are God's new chosen people, sir?" Taylor responded.

"Oh, yes!" Polk replied with enthusiasm.

"That God intends for his people to have the land to the west of us?" Taylor continued.

"And so much more." Polk grinned.

Taylor contemplated his next answer. "Well, I do believe that God is always with us. And that God would not want any blood spilled on either land, and he wants us to be at peace with one another." General Taylor paused. "But if the security of the United States is at stake, then I will heed *her* call and protect our great country."

President Polk got up from his chair and headed toward General Taylor to put his hand on Taylor's shoulder.

"That is precisely why I asked you to come here today. You see, I believe you are here for the protection of our country. I want you to maintain the peace between two neighboring countries. I want you in command at Fort Texas, just north of Matamoros."

"But sir," Taylor said, trying not to sound rude, "that is Mexican territory. The Mexicans could, and will, see this as an invasion from the United States."

"I do see your point. That is why I sent a political envoy to Mexico City to clear up our territory situation."

"Sir?" Taylor questioned.

"To prevent any misunderstandings there could be between two neighbors. Besides, we will offer Mexico a substantial amount of currency for their land to the west and in the end. Each nation will prosper. And your presence is only to ensure our nation's interest," Polk said with much conviction.

Taylor hesitated and then replied, "Well then, that is great news, Mr. President. I shall go where you need me most, and I will make the appropriate arrangements."

"Thank you, General Taylor. I knew I had the right man for the job."

As soon as the general left the office, the two remaining men continued their discussion. Dallas addressed the president. "Mr. President, if Mexico does not agree with your offer, they might take General Taylor's presence as hostile."

Polk walked to the main window and saw the general leaving the grounds. He noticed the general looking back at the White House in an unsettling way. The general did not see the president, nor could he hear him.

Polk whispered his response as if he were whispering it to General Taylor himself. "I can only hope so."

Outside, a young man ran toward General Taylor. His name was Ulysses S. Grant. Grant had just graduated from West Point at the age of twenty-four. He was eager to learn all he could from General Taylor. He had heard all the stories of the wars General Taylor had been in.

"Well, General, how did it go, sir?"

Taylor replied in a somber tone, "It's a bad situation that just got worse."

"Sir?"

"The president wants us to deploy to south Texas," Taylor said with a lousy grin.

"Is that so bad?" Grant asked.

"In this case, yes. But remember, son, it will always be our duty to serve this country. So we must ensure that we do everything in our power to safeguard her security—whether or not we agree with the decision made by men in power."

A confused Grant replied, "General, you did say that the president wants us in south Texas?"

"To ensure our border is intact."

"So he wants us on the borderline of the Nueces River?"

Taylor's grin was more comical now.

"I'd say about three hundred miles more south."

Grant was confused but replied, "Isn't that Mexican territory, sir?"

"Right above Matamoros," Taylor confirmed.

Grant knew not to ask so many questions. "I see. Well then, with the general's permission, I shall get the troops ready, sir." Grant saluted Taylor.

"Very well, Lieutenant," Taylor replied as he saluted back.

As Grant left General Taylor, the general continued walking, contemplating his actions for the future. With his mind preoccupied, he did not notice a young man approaching. He greeted the general with his arm outstretched.

"General Taylor. It's quite the honor and pleasure to finally meet you, sir, face to face," stated the young man.

Taylor recognized the man but failed to remember his name.

"The pleasure is all mine. You're one of the new young congressman, correct? I am sorry; I cannot place your name, sir."

"Abraham Lincoln, General. We met at a congressional dinner a few weeks ago. It's a pleasure to run into you once again, General."

"Please, sir, you flatter me, and I do recall your name. I also believe I have read some of your material. Apparently someone wrote an article in the *Sangamon Journal*, mocking a certain James Shields?" Taylor said with a smirk.

Lincoln responded, in a futile effort to deny it, "Well, that article was supposed to be anonymous."

"This is Washington; nothing is a secret. Did he not challenge you to a duel recently?"

Lincoln was rattled but composed himself and replied, "Yes, I chose cavalry broadswords, for I was the challenger. But it never flourished."

Taylor admired Lincoln for his sincerity and responded, "I heard it was called off."

"Yes, General. It seemed best for both parties not to pursue the issue."

"A wise decision, for his sake. I might have need for him in the future," Taylor replied with a sincere smile.

"Yes, I suppose." Anxious to leave, Lincoln excused himself. "Well then, good day to you, General."

"Thank you, sir. And to you."

3

On a ranch in north Texas, a man by the name of John Clifford was feeding his livestock. As he fed his animals, he noticed his children running across his acreage. He had two boys, six and twelve years old. He smiled with fulfillment as they ran across the plains. For John, it seemed as if had taken an eternity to finally find this kind of happiness. He had been a soldier for a long time and had seen the effects of war. He had fought alongside General Taylor in the Black Hawk War and Second Seminole War. Those were wars he would like to soon forget.

John Clifford was also a religious man. He made a promise to God that if God would protect him through the wars and battles, he would be a just and righteous father, husband, and soldier. John had also gone against the norm in his town by not owning a slave. The South still had strong views of owning slaves, but Clifford's views condemned the practice.

As he continued to concentrate on his task at hand, his wife, Sarah, came up from behind and hugged him. He was taken aback and said, "Darling, what are you doing?"

"What? I can't show my old man some good old country affection?" his wife replied.

A little embarrassed, John responded, "But honey, you know I've been working all day. I smell worse than the hogs."

She took in a big whiff and jokingly replied, "Well, I think the smell suits you."

"Are you saying that I smell just as bad as a hog?" John inquired with annoyance.

She broke his embrace as he turned to her. She was positioned in a grapple stance. "Oh, no. If I said that, I would be insulting the hogs."

John grinned and went to a grapple position as well. "Oh, really?"

He took his wife, picked her up, and gently laid her to the ground. They laughed and stared at each other for a second as John leaned in to kiss her. The kiss was as soft as the wind caressing a flower. Not five seconds later, their children came running and landed on John's back.

His eldest, Roberto, said, "You leave Mama alone."

"Yeah, Mama alone," John's youngest, Michael, agreed.

John leaped up with both boys around his body. He made sure he had a good grip on both of them and replied, "Oh, so you are both taking her side, I see."

The boys struggled to get a grip on their father, but it was no use. He was bigger and stronger. John was showing off now. "Not bad for an old man, huh?"

"Daddy, you're not old. Just smelly," Roberto responded.

John was shocked. Not so much at what Roberto said, but at the fact that it made their mother laugh even harder.

"Oh, now you've done it," John replied. He wrestled his sons in the mud.

Then they all began to laugh, except John's wife. "That's all good and fun, but don't even think about coming into the house with all that mud on your shoes."

They all replied in unison, as if they were in a vaudeville play, "Yes, Mother."

As they continued to play, John's wife headed back to the house and suddenly saw dust rising from the distance.

She shouted out to John, "John, John, someone's coming."

They saw a uniformed courier riding like the wind. He was holding onto his satchel, which contained a telegram meant for Colonel Clifford. Once the young soldier reached the couple, he tried to speak but noticed a smell. His expression was comical as he began to speak. "Sorry for the intrusion, Colonel, but—"

John's face was beginning to turn red with frustration as he interrupted the soldier. "Boy, you know full well I have a leave of absence that lasts for one more month."

"Yes, Colonel, but this is urgent. It's from General Taylor himself." The soldier handed John the telegram.

Sarah could not contain herself. "John, what is it?"

"I've been called back. It seems there is a situation brewing in south Texas. General Taylor wants all his men to aid the troops and train some volunteers."

"Volunteers? Well, how big is this situation? Will it be like the Alamo?"

"Can't really say, but if Taylor is using volunteers, it could be." John then addressed the young soldier. "You, soldier, go on ahead and water your horse."

"But sir, are we not leaving immediately?"

"My wife made supper, and it would be an insult to leave now. Besides, by the looks of it, your horse may need some rest. As soon as we finish our meal, we will leave."

"Yes, sir." The young soldier got off his horse, and John's eldest son led him to the barn.

Roberto addressed the soldier. "This way."

As John's family was finishing their meal, an uncomfortable silence had descended upon them. John was used to chatter around the dinner table, but tonight, the mood was very somber.

The young soldier broke the silence. "Boy, that was amazing food, Mrs. Clifford."

Sarah responded, "Why, thank you, Private."

John tried to join the conversation. "It truly was a wonderful supper, dear; it will be a while till I eat something like that again."

Sarah responded, "Thank you, dear." She excused herself and left to the bedroom.

John looked at his boys and then addressed the young soldier. "I think it is time to take our leave." He then looked at his sons. "Boys, why don't you help Private Smith get his horse ready, as well as mine?"

John's eldest son answered, "Very well, Father. Let's go, Michael."

The two boys led the young soldier to the stables. John got up and made his way to the bedroom. He saw his wife finish packing up his things for his departure. She spoke firmly. "How long do you think you'll be gone?"

"Probably a couple of months. Maybe a year at the most," John replied as he tried to comfort Sarah.

She then began to slowly break down. She spoke with a slight tremble in her voice. "I'm so scared, John."

He embraced her and tried to comfort her. "You know, I'm not used to seeing you like this. You're the strong one, remember?"

"I try to be—for you, for our children. I guess I just have a bad feeling about this one. I don't know what it is." Sarah was starting to have doubts about John's departure.

"Well, you know, Manuel and Maria and their whole family will keep an eye on you if you need anything."

"And you? Who's going to keep an eye out for you?"

John looked her straight in her eyes and said with conviction, "Nothing could ever, ever keep me from you or our boys. Not in this lifetime. I'll be fine, darling. There's nothing to worry about. God will be with me, and he will protect me."

"You're a good man, a God-fearing man. You have a wife who loves you and two wonderful children who adore you."

"I thought I was comforting you."

Sarah smiled and kissed her husband. "You did, and I love you for it."

"I love you too. You know, I am the luckiest man alive."

Clifford's son Roberto walked in. He looked up at his father and said, "Pa, I finished getting your horse ready, and I…" Roberto got all choked up.

"Yes, son?"

"Just be careful, Pa, and come back soon." Roberto reached and embraced his father. Roberto tried secretly to put something in his father's pocket as they finished embracing. "Promise not to look at it right away. Only look at it when you miss us the most."

John was curious and answered, "What is it?"

"Just promise me, OK?"

John looked at his son. He saw Roberto's eyes water and whispered, "I promise."

Michael interrupted the moment and said, "Be careful."

With a great big smile, John lifted his youngest up to his shoulders and said, "I will, boys. Now remember, you are the men of this household while I'm gone. But also remember to mind your mama. Understood?"

The boys nodded their heads and saluted.

"Those are my good little soldiers." John saluted them back. John looked at his wife as he put his son down and lifted his luggage. "Bye, Sarah, my love. You are in my heart always."

"God be with you always."

They embraced one last time. John got on his horse and began to ride off. When he had ridden out far enough, he took out the piece of paper Roberto had given him. It was a drawing of their farm. He and his wife were riding horses as the two boys fed the chickens. John smiled and put the drawing back into his pocket.

4

El General

The next morning, over the great expanse of trees and mountains surrounding the Castle of Chapultepec, a figure walked through the halls. The sunlight broke through the castle's windows and arcs and fell on the figure. His name was General Jose Mariano Monterde, but the majority of people called him *El General.* Though he was a pleasant-looking man, Monterde had fought many battles, and the distress was visible on his face. Monterde was known to not show his emotions on the battlefield, whether contentment or disgust. As he walked through the halls, which was something he did every morning, he was stopped by one of the cadets at the school, Juan Escutia.

Juan approached Monterde with caution and saluted his commander. "Morning, sir!"

The commander saluted back. "At ease, soldier."

Nervously, Juan responded, "Permission to speak, sir?"

"Permission granted."

"Sir, I've done all my morning duties and would like to have a word!"

"Very well, Cadet. Follow me," Monterde instructed.

As Monterde walked into his office, the young cadet followed him deferentially. When Monterde reached his desk, he attempted to take off his coat. The young cadet immediately assisted him. As Monterde sat down, he noticed the cadet was at attention. "At ease, Cadet."

"Thank you, sir!" Juan Escutia replied as he waited for the general to sit first.

Monterde began. "What is so important that you needed to see me so early in the morning?"

"Well, sir." Juan hesitated for a moment and then continued. "I have heard many rumors and would like to know if the general has received any word of *his* whereabouts?"

"Ah! Well, son." Monterde paused for a second but then resumed. "I have heard *he* is now in Chihuahua."

"Is that all, sir?" Juan cautiously inquired.

Monterde hesitated again. "No…"

Juan wanted to know everything and pled with the general. "Sir, please."

"I heard that before he headed to Chihuahua, he raided a village and attacked some Indians along the Rio Grande. It's reported that twenty-three men, twelve women, and six children were killed in the raid," Monterde responded reluctantly.

Juan looked down as if he already knew the answer. He then stood at attention. "Sir, thank you for your candor."

The young man saluted his superior. As he was leaving the general's office, he saw Juan de la Barrera seated in a chair. Juan had been in the military since the age of twelve. This was a very big privilege for military children, especially for the son of the famous General Ignacio Maria de la Barrera. His father was well known as one of the great military minds of the time. A day did not go by that Juan was not reminded of who his father was. All eyes were on Juan, and he was expected to follow in his father's footsteps. Juan was the type of cadet every other student wanted to be. At age nineteen, he was currently one of the oldest cadets in school. This was his last year at the academy. Since there were many cadets named Juan, they referred to him simply as Bara. As Juan Escutia left Monterde's office, the two boys acknowledged each other. Bara just stared at Juan Escutia. Juan, in return, smiled back. Before he could react, Bara was called into the general's office. Bara got up and entered. His salute was ready for the commander.

The general saluted back and spoke. "Have a seat, soldier."

Bara took his seat and replied, "Thank you, General."

"How many times do we have to do this, son?" General Monterde asked cynically.

"Enough times so I eventually learn my lesson?" Bara answered optimistically.

Monterde grinned when he heard Bara's reply, but returned to his usual constrained demeanor. "Just because you can put a smile on some of the cadets' faces, that doesn't give you latitude with the professors, Bara."

"My apologies, General. I suppose I like to put a smile on people's faces."

"You did not put one on Professor Tomas this morning," Monterde responded sharply.

"Sir, the professor in question was judging me by who my father is. I will not be identified by him or be linked to *his* accomplishments. It seems as if I will always be in his shadow.

We are two separate and contradictory people," Bara replied firmly.

Monterde seemed to agree with Bara. "I am aware of that. Nevertheless, these professors are your superiors, and you will respect each and every one of them."

Bara looked at the general with frustration. "Fine. Is there anything else, General?" grumbled Bara.

"Son, please don't ruffle my feathers so early in the morning," Monterde responded with a commanding tone.

Bara realized his mistake. "Sorry. I beg your pardon, General."

"My job is to make you the finest soldier."

"But that's not what I want, sir," Bara responded.

Monterde agreed. "I understand. I have read your papers on the strategies of war. Your talent for warfare is superb."

Bara, trying to restrain himself, spoke softly. "But sir, I want to use my brain for creating, not destroying."

Monterde stared with curiosity. "Is that what you think your father does?"

Bara just stared at the general, afraid that any answer would upset him.

"I see. I've also read your paper on the effect of organics on wildlife. I think you can be a successful scientist," replied Monterde.

"Thank you, sir."

"That is why I need you to harness your anger when people mention your father. Remember, you are on probation. Therefore, I have a special assignment for you," Monterde said encouragingly.

"How special, sir?"

For someone who did not show emotion, Monterde had a gratified look on his face. "It's special enough to distract you, and help you deal with that anger. I want you to mentor a student."

"Mentor?"

Monterde gave the following order. "I want you to give the student a positive direction and advice on becoming a better solder. That is all."

"Don't you mean a nanny, sir?" Bara said, annoyed.

"Interpret it anyway you want. I need you to stay out of trouble during your remaining time here."

Bara seemed a little annoyed with Monterde's assignment. Monterde resumed. "My decision is final. I suggest you get used to the idea right away. Do I make myself clear, Lieutenant?"

Bara realized it was an order. "Sir, yes, sir."

Monterde, satisfied with Bara's response, replied, "See the secretary; he will give you the name of the student in question. Dismissed."

Bara stood up and saluted his commander. He left the office, and the secretary gave him the name of his project. Bara was dumbfounded when he read who it was. Baffled, Bara moaned, "Him?"

5

The view from the Castle of Chapultepec was majestic. No matter where you looked, it was beautiful. One particular view was of the quarters where the cadets stayed. In one room, a young man named Francisco Marquez was writing a letter at his desk. Francisco's father had died at a very young age. Francisco's mother decided that if she married an officer, her son would have a chance at a future. She married a captain of the cavalry named Francisco Ortiz. She hoped his new stepfather could give her son some direction in his life. Being related to a military family almost guaranteed an education; you could be admitted to the academy instantly if you had military relations. Francisco's stepfather encouraged him to be more militant, but Francisco's demeanor was calm and low key. A real serene presence could be found in him. It was a trait his stepfather did not like, but young Francisco did not know what direction he wanted to go. Although his stepfather wanted him to be more militant, he found himself drawn to a theological career rather than a military one. Yet, at sixteen years old, career choices and decisions were new for Francisco.

Young Francisco was finishing his letter when Juan came in violently, returning from the general's office. "Oh, sorry about that. I thought all the cadets were at chore duty," Juan apologized, realizing that he was not alone.

"That's OK. I finished my duties early so I could write a brief letter to my mother."

"My, what a good little soldier," Juan said mockingly.

Defiantly, Francisco responded, "Since my father died, my mother wants me to write to her whenever I feel alone."

"Sorry. Did you know your father very well?" Juan apologized, honestly. He then saw a large knife on Francisco's bunk. He got close to the knife and picked it up.

"Not really. He died when I was very young," Francisco said in a somber tone.

Without really thinking, Juan responded, "Count your blessings."

"What do you mean?" Francisco was beginning to get upset.

"Nothing, never mind. This was your father's knife?"

Francisco began to calm down. "Yes, it is one of the few things I have left of him. That and his cross. I feel close to him whenever I hold his cross. Funny how these two things couldn't be more different. Yet I need them both, I guess."

Juan set the knife back down and tried to change the subject. "So, why do you feel alone?"

"Well, it's just, lately—"

Suddenly, the boys heard the bell ring for the second class to begin.

"We don't want to be late. I'll see you later, maybe at lunch-time," Juan said.

"You mean I can sit with you and your friends at the dining hall?" Francisco asked hopefully.

"Hell no. Just that I will see you at lunch. Later, *cabron*," Juan said as he left the room laughing. Francisco ran out of the room so he wouldn't be late for class.

6

Hidden Agenda

An envoy was approaching Mexico City, and the dust rose up into the sky. The roads outside of the city were not paved, and signs of dusk had begun to appear. The envoy had a total of five wagons, one right after the other. The middle wagon was occupied by the Slidell company. John Slidell was a Louisiana politician who had been appointed commissioner of Mexico by President Polk. He had been a big supporter of Polk during the presidential election of 1844. President Polk had sent Slidell on a mission, and, as the envoy continued its approach to the city limits, Slidell was in deep conversation with fellow politicians.

"So, you have specific instructions from the president?" one of the politicians said.

Slidell responded matter-of-factly, "Well he has trust in me that everything will go as planned."

"Because you know the tension in Texas is mounting," a second politician interrupted.

Slidell responded, "Well, that's why we are here—to alleviate that tension with millions of dollars."

"And what does this trade entail?" The second politician was now curious.

"Five million for some of the northern territories. For California, the price is unlimited. But the president would like us to keep the amount under twenty-five million." Slidell chuckled.

"Well, the offer should suffice the Mexicans, for it's twice what we paid for the Louisiana Purchase forty years ago," a politician replied.

"Yes, but, when that land was purchased, it had Indians on it," Slidell responded.

"Indians, Mexicans—I still do not see the difference. And, pray tell, what else would the president have us do?" a fellow politician replied.

Slidell cleared his throat. "To make it clear that they recognize the border of Texas will be to the Rio Grande."

"What happened to the Nueces border?" the second politician inquired.

"Apparently, the president thinks we can just bully'em down," Slidell responded with authority. All the politicians laughed.

"I see his point," one of the politicians chimed in.

"We should just take it like we did Texas," the second politician said.

Slidell responded, smiling, "Yes, but this time we have more eyes focused upon us. We have to give them the chance to do the right thing. All we want is to avoid confrontation, or, at least, give the appearance of it. So it is in their best interest to accept what we have to offer."

Still another politician had a question. "Mr. Slidell, when we purchase the Northern Territories from Mexico, will the Mexican government accept our terms?"

"Well, the president said it wouldn't be easy," Slidell responded.

They all laughed. Their coach reached its destination. Slidell looked out and addressed his fellow politicians. "Now remember, gentleman, get a full night's rest. We will need it as we prepare for our negotiations tomorrow. Then we will wait for an official meeting with the Mexican Congress."

7

Back at the Castle of Chapultepec, cadets were training at the shooting range. Fernando and Bara were loading their weapons. Having shot since he was five, Fernando was an expert. There was no dialogue between them until curiosity got the better of Fernando. "So, how did it go with the general?"

"Oh, you know, the usual," Bara said casually.

"Bara, when are you going to listen?" Fernando replied in a lecture manner.

"Oh, like you are such a good soldier?" Bara mocked Fernando.

"A good student, I must admit I am not. A good soldier, on the other hand, you bet your ass. I am the best at what I do."

Fernando finished reloading his rifle. He took aim, shot his rifle, and hit the bull's-eye.

"Damn, don't you ever miss?"

"Once. But I didn't like the feeling," Fernando responded conceitedly. "Now, don't change the subject on me. What kind of punishment did the general give you?" Fernando waited as he reloaded his rifle once more.

Bara tried to give a convincing response. "Well, it's kind of complicated."

"What, is he going to ship you off to the army already?" Fernando replied with a silly gesture.

"No, he just wants me to help a cadet out. Like a special project. It's very prestigious." Fernando just stared at Bara and waited for the truth to come out. Bara confessed, "I have to make him officer material. Satisfied?"

"Why go to you, then?" Fernando replied, holding in his laughter.

"And why not me?" answered Bara, irritated.

"You, as a mentor? Get serious. I mean, two years ago, of course. You were the model cadet. Everyone wanted to be you, including me. But you haven't been the same since the incident. It feels like you changed somehow. And since then, everything you do, you don't take seriously," Fernando said desperately.

"Why are you getting so upset? If anything, it should be me who is upset. You know what they took from me. I can't forgive them, or him, for that. And to top it off, I'm stuck watching over this cadet," Bara responded with a defensive tone.

"Listen, Bara. All I know is that they didn't grant you your promotion to be a science officer and that your father had something to do with it. As a good friend, I did not want to push the subject. But I know there's more to it."

"That is precisely why I haven't told you everything. I want you to live your life without any influence from me. You have this purist idea of military life. And I, for one, will not destroy your ideology like they did mine. No matter if I oppose it or not."

"Your father really messed you up," Fernando said.

"Listen, Fernando, I'm not like you or the other military officers. Many of the professors and our director have seen war and are just like my father. War changes a person. The difference between me and them is that, in the end, I just want to be happy with the person I've chosen to be and not have it be chosen for me. Listen, I don't mean to give you a hard time. But what I wanted the most was taken away from me. I don't want the life my father leads. I will take charge and not let it take me like it did my father."

"I…just want you to be comfortable with your remaining time here," Fernando said sadly.

"I'm trying, but I guess I do overreact at times. I just don't want to impose my problems on you or anybody."

Fernando saw Bara's distress and, with a calming tone, replied, "Well then, if you can't confide in me completely, then find someone you can confide in, that's all. You can't keep all this resentment inside you. You will be graduating soon. Remember, that incident was two years ago. Let it go. You want to keep it all in; that's fine. But it's boiling over onto the rest of us. You continuously belittle everyone who reminds you of your father—the professors especially, giving them a hard time." Fernando looked at Bara with empathy.

"I know. I will try harder to let it go." Fernando looked at Bara with hesitation. To reassure his friend, Bara added, "I will. Promise."

"Well then, since you will try, I will help you out with this special project of yours."

Bara started to smile. "Fair enough. So, are we still friends?"

"It will take a whole lot more than you just being a *cabron* for me not to be your friend."

Bara stood up and said, "We live together; we fight together."

Fernando smiled as he replied. "Friends. See you tonight."

8

Mr. Slidell was staying at one of the most prestigious hotels in Mexico City, El Pedregal. He walked vigorously across his room in anticipation. The hotel had given him and his fellow politicians one of the biggest rooms they had. Several men were talking to one another in an adjacent room. Suddenly, there was a knock at the door. As it swung open, several Mexican officials were standing outside the door. Mr. Slidell invited them all to come in. The leader of the group addressed Mr. Slidell. "Mr. Slidell, what a pleasure, sir."

"The pleasure is all mine," Slidell responded.

After the men concluded their meet and greet, the lead Mexican official walked toward Mr. Slidell to converse in private. "I was able to arrange a meeting with many important officials, Mr. Slidell, but not with Congress. You see, there is much speculation on why you are here. Rumors, really."

"Well, if this is how it is done in Mexico, very well. Let's not keep them waiting. Let's try to eradicate these rumors. I have had my share of rumors," Slidell replied abruptly.

As the lead Mexican official began to leave the room with the other officials, Mr. Slidell turned his attention to his fellow politicians.

"There has been a change in plans, but rest assured I've debated many times in Congress. How difficult can it be to enlighten a bunch of Mex...other nationalities?" Slidell said to his cohorts as he noticed the Mexican official waiting for them.

They were led to a great hall. Slidell heard a small ruckus that eventually got louder and louder as he neared the entrance. As Slidell came to the end of the hall, he saw many men arguing in a round room, but they all stopped suddenly when they saw Mr. Slidell. His entourage followed him in.

One of the distinguished gentlemen, who had been arguing, approached Mr. Slidell and said, "Mr. John Slidell, we have convened this meeting for the sole purpose of crushing the nasty rumors that you are here to purchase our country and to talk about borderlines that have currently been crossed by your country. Once you clear up these rumors, we can continue to grant you a meeting with Congress."

With an arrogant attitude, Slidell addressed the Mexican politicians. "Of course, gentlemen. Thank you for your attention to this matter. Well, many of you have heard of the recent trouble in Texas. I am authorized, by the president of the United States, to make your government an offer."

"What kind of offer, sir?" a second Mexican official interrupted.

"It is the kind of offer that Mexico needs right now. Gentleman, we have noticed that your country has suffered much these past years with revolution, poverty, and the loss of Texas. Now, we know that your treasury is nearly depleted. We currently find ourselves in a crucial state where two neighbors must come together to resolve their problems. We recently resolved the one with Britain, and why not, now, with Mexico? All we want to do is to ease your pain and relieve some of your pressure by purchasing your northern territories. But, first, we need you to recognize that the border of Texas is to be drawn at the edge of the Rio Grande. If you do this, I am in a position to offer Mexico a substantial amount of money for the *land* I just mentioned. What say you?"

Many of the Mexican diplomats and congressmen couldn't contain their anger and were about to address Mr. Slidell when diplomat Donaciano Medina addressed him. The room got quiet once again, for all of the men respected this older gentleman.

"Even if we were to consider such a proposition, who is to say that the United States wouldn't want to expand the Texas border all the way south? Let's say, to Panama or wherever the US would want such a border. Now, you say you want to purchase half our country. And you and your president have the audacity to offer us a bribe? No, gentleman, we will not begin to sell our souls for thirty pieces of silver, nor those of an entire country. Mexico has lost many of its citizens in the ultimate sacrifice. Their blood was spilled for this land, for their freedom. Their sacrifice would be in vain if we just sold it. This country, true, has had its share of problems in the past, but they were resolved. And with our current ones, we will find solutions as well. Mexico will do this without the help of the United States. So we regret to inform you that there will be no meeting with Congress. I do believe that I share the same opinion as the rest of my fellow diplomats when I say that there will be no sale today."

"Gentlemen, you must understand, I will not make such a generous offer again. Will you reconsider?" Slidell responded with disdain in his voice.

The diplomat Medina replied with a powerful tone, "Tell your President Polk that Mexico is not for sale and that the border for Texas is at the Nueces River. If you cross the border, it will be interpreted as a sign of invasion. If so, we will act accordingly. Believe me when I say, Mexico will not back down to you or any other country again. We have fought the Spanish and gained our independence. So much was given for our independence; we will not lose it so easily. If you breach Mexico's borders, we will defend ourselves, and we will be victorious."

Slidell felt shock and then anger, yet he refrained from showing his true emotion.

"Very well. I shall inform my president of your decision as soon as possible. I take my leave," Slidell said in a pompous tone.

Many of the Mexican congressmen saw Slidell's disrespect and tried to stop him and his entourage from leaving.

Congressman Medina realized this action would only encourage the United States to declare war on Mexico, and he addressed his colleagues. "Let them continue on their way out. We have said our piece."

Mr. Slidell's entourage continued to exit nervously. All the Mexican officials hoped that what they had said would be enough for the United States to halt its advance. Only time would tell.

9

Back at the Castle of Chapultepec, Bara and Fernando were sneaking their way through the dorm halls early in the morning. Fernando Montes de Oca, nineteen years old, had been friends with Bara for a while now. Both young men shared a common bond; they had joined the military at a very young age, and both had reputable parents who had served in the military. It was unavoidable that they would forge a friendship. As the two continued to walk in the dark, they tried to be as quiet as they could be.

Fernando broke the silence with a whisper. "Four o'clock in the morning! What the hell are we doing up so early?" he asked groggily.

"I told you already. Monterde wants *us* to be a mentor to this young cadet."

"Us? I don't remember being in the general's office. Besides, you make a better nanny than I would," Fernando replied, annoyed.

"Hey, aren't we friends to the end?" Bara asked, as if he didn't know the answer already.

"Well, yes, but to drag me out of bed at four o'clock in the morning? We need to reevaluate this friendship," Fernando said sharply.

"Listen, if I can push this cadet hard enough, he will ask the general to replace me, and then I'm free. So if the general wants me to make this cadet into a model soldier here at the academy, I'll make him the best one we've ever had."

"This is so bad," Fernando groaned.

"What, my idea?" Bara asked.

"No, the idea that you think you're smarter than the general."

"I know what I'm doing," Bara said with conviction.

"Famous last words. Fine, let's get on with it," Fernando said as he started to roll his eyes.

The two cadets snuck into the quarters of Juan Escutia. They moved like predators right before the kill. They heard Escutia snoring under his bedcovers. All of a sudden, the only sound in the room besides the snoring was that of the two cadets snickering. Trying to contain their laughter, the two got closer to Juan Escutia to wake him in an abrupt manner, just to see the look on his face. They slowly climbed on top of his bed and began to jump up and down. Much to their surprise, all that came from under the covers was a small groan. Stunned by this reaction, the two boys began to jump even higher until they heard a loud crack and realized they had broken the bed frame. To their surprise, the cadet under the covers was Francisco, Escutia's roommate.

"What?" Francisco said, sitting up. "What's wrong? Are we at war?" As soon as he said this, he went back to sleep.

The only ones more confused than Francisco were the two cadets.

"We're in the right room, right?" Fernando asked in bewilderment.

"Yeah, but where is Juan Escutia?" Bara replied.

Before anyone could answer, Juan Escutia emerged from one of the side doors leading to the hallway. While adjusting his uniform, he addressed the two cadets. "Good morning, Lieutenants. I see you woke up my roommate."

"Good morning? Is that all you have to say, Cadet?" Bara said angrily.

Bara and Fernando climbed off the bed and approached Juan Escutia.

"And why is your roommate in *your* bunk?" Fernando asked Juan.

"Well, I told him we needed to switch beds because it was a military exercise, something about misguiding the enemy. But I pretty much could have told him anything, and he would have done it."

Juan's answer did not sit well with Bara. Bara replied without hesitation, "Well, since you are so well prepared for guiding or misguiding, how about we guide you straight to the stables for manure duty this morning?" Bara gloated and added, "What do you think, Fernando?"

With a smile on his face, Fernando replied, "Oh, I think that's an excellent idea."

"Permission to speak," Juan asked Bara.

"Go ahead, Cadet," Bara responded.

"I did your—I mean those chores were done last night, sir. Perhaps the lieutenants would like me to do some other useless chore? Or may I suggest we use the lieutenant's expertise on this cadet?"

"Don't get smart with me, Cadet. But, out of curiosity, what did you have in mind?"

"I could use your help in my cavalry attacks, sir."

"And?" Bara asked with hesitation.

"Well, the whole school knows you are the best rider there is, sir!"

Bara looked at Fernando to make sure he had heard what Juan had just said. Bara's chest was all puffed out, and he responded, "Oh, I see. You think that if you flatter me enough, I will just go ahead and teach you what I know?"

"Well, yeah," Fernando answered for Juan.

Bara responded, "Sad but true. Fine. Meet me at the stables in one hour. And if anyone asks, it was my all idea."

"Yes, sir," Juan responded with a small smirk.

10

True Colors

As a cool breeze swept through the White House, leaves were scattered over the White House steps. The wind brushed through the trees. Silence was abruptly overtaken by the sound of men chattering. There was a congestion of men standing around, engaged in conversations. Many of the men were drinking tea, while others paced up and down the room. For the most part, the mood seemed optimistic, but there were those who seemed to be uneasy. A courier rode toward the White House grounds. He leaped off his horse and walked toward the front door, between two very large columns. The courier was greeted by soldiers.

"I have urgent news from the Slidell envoy that must be brought to President Polk's attention."

"Wait here," one of the soldiers replied.

As the soldier went inside, the other struck up a conversation. "Where did you ride from, boy?"

"I rode straight from the telegram's express sir, with specific orders from the president!"

Suddenly the door opened, and a different soldier emerged. "The president will see you."

The soldier led the courier to the president's office, and the courier looked around with insecurity as he took in the grand nature of the huge room. He was then left alone, standing nervously. He seemed only to be focused on the back of the large chair behind the desk. The chair began to rotate.

President Polk addressed the young courier. "What news do you have, boy?"

The courier managed to address the president. "A letter for you from the Slidell envoy, Mr. President."

President Polk smiled. "Could you read the telegram for me, please?"

Surprised by President Polk's request, he began to read. "Dear Mr. President. Stop. In the conversation we had earlier, you were right. Stop. Depend on it, sir. Stop. We can never get along with the Mexicans until we've given them a proper drubbing. Stop."

Amused by the telegram, the president nonchalantly replied, "Is that all?"

"Yes, sir," the boy said nervously.

"My dear boy," the president said as he reached into his desk to retrieve a sealed written message, "please take this telegram and deliver it with priority. It is for General Taylor."

11

Once a royal residence, the Castle of Chapultepec had been transformed into one of the finest educational and military schools in Mexico, yet no classroom was needed for Cavalry Tactics 101. The class was held on the west side of the castle grounds. Two cadets were sitting on a fence admiring their friend's riding. One of the cadets sitting on the fence was Agustin Melgar, and seated next to him was Fernando. As Agustin and Fernando talked, they watched riders go by. They both commented on Bara's riding technique. Bara drew out his sword and, with a swift glide, cut the top of his target, which had been placed on a pole. Bara then rode back to Juan Escutia. He instructed Juan to mimic what he just performed.

While Bara continued to instruct Juan on proper Calvary tactics, Agustin asked Fernando a question. "So, what do you think about this new tutor program?" Agustin began to smile.

"Well, if I were to tutor anyone, it would be for only one person—Vicente's sister."

Agustin was not amused by Fernando's comment. But before Agustin could say anything, Vicente, who had been standing behind them the whole time, unnoticed, snuck up on Fernando and lifted his foot right over the fence, forcing him to fall over. Some other cadets witnessed the act and busted into laugher.

Vicente was very protective of his sister because his father, a first lieutenant in the cavalry, was away for long periods of time. Vicente's and Agustin's parents were very close, for they had all been stationed at the same command post for years. Agustin knew better than to mention Vicente's sister around cadets.

As Fernando began to pick himself up and dust himself off, Bara started to laugh. "Serves you right. Don't know what you did, but you probable deserved it," Bara yelled at Fernando.

"*Ay, caramba*, Vicente looks sore. What made him do that?" Juan interrupted.

"If I know Vicente, it probably concerns his sister. He is so protective. And why not? She is very beautiful. I suggest you don't mention his sister, or least not in front of him."

"Thanks for the warning," Juan said, shaking his head.

"No problem. OK, let's begin again." Bara continued to instruct Juan, but he realized that Juan was not performing the correct technique. "No, you're holding the reins too tight. No, now you're overcompensating. It sends the horse the wrong message."

"I think I got it." Juan began to charge.

"No, you don't. Just be lucky he doesn't kick you—"

Before Bara could finish his sentence, the horse kicked Juan off his back.

The cadets roared with laughter.

Bara tried to contain his laughter as he ran to see if Juan was all right.

"I told you so," Bara said, grinning.

"Yeah, yeah," Juan replied as he rubbed his behind.

"Look, I have to be honest with you. I really did not want to be in this mentor situation. And I don't think you wanted it as well. But, in a way, I'm kind of glad it happened. It's good to know that when I'm gone, the school will be in the good hands of cadets like you."

"Ha, you really don't know me. How do you know I'm such a good cadet?" Juan said, testing Bara.

"Let's just say, I heard from a reliable source that you have a lot of potential. Listen, I just had the worst two years of my life, but then it dawned on me. I just need to let it go and concentrate on the goods things in life. Believe it or not, the goodwill always outweighs the bad—if, and only if, you have the courage to try to find the good and the beauty in life. Last night I was walking in the courtyard in the middle of the night and stared at our flag on top of the citadel. And I saw the beauty in what our flag represents. I realized what our forefathers fought for long ago, and what I fight for now."

"What?" Juan asked.

"Freedom—the freedom to live our own lives and to do what is right. And since I am leaving, I'll have it soon."

"So you're not free now?" Juan responded, as he was now curious.

"I'd like to think that I'm almost there." Bara smiled.

"I...think I know what you're talking about. I'm trying to free myself as well."

"From what?"

"Something my father did, or is doing. And if we are comparing fathers, yours is perfect."

"Is that what you think?" Bara asked Juan.

"Why, yes. The famous General De La Barrera who led the Mexican Army against the Spaniards," Juan said with conviction.

"Oh, those famous stories. And what else do you know?" Bara continued to question Juan.

"That's all, I guess. He's brave and an excellent commander."

"And very demanding. Since I was twelve, I have been groomed to be the next generation of military officer. I was the perfect student. But that wasn't enough. He kept pushing and pushing me to be more like him. But men like him know only one thing, and that's all they know. Pride. He eventually became the most well-known general anyone had ever seen or heard of. Suffice to say, he was not at home very often. And if he was to be the best general there was, he had to sacrifice being a good father. If I wanted my father's attention, I had to become the perfect soldier. But, during that time, I began to realize I didn't want to be anything like him, cold and distant. I discovered I am very fond of science. I like to discover new things. Not destroy them. So I decided to be a science officer."

"And your father was OK with that?"

"Well, when I solicited to be a science officer for higher education, I was denied."

"Why?" Juan was now intrigued.

"They wouldn't be specific, but I can only speculate that it had something to do with my father. I can't say I'm all that surprised. I even confronted him; he just said it was probably for the best and that I wouldn't have done well in science. It was the longest talk I had had with my father in three years. I even tried confronting the administration. They just told me I didn't have the qualifications to be a science officer, but I could move up in rank for military tactics. I guess they just want me to be a mindless soldier who takes orders. Just like my father."

Juan tried to speak but decided not to.

Bara began to speak again, since the silence was becoming uncomfortable. "Well, I guess that's why I have been giving the professors here such a hard time. Deep down, I know it's not their fault. It's my father's—God, how I hate him. But, in the end, I guess I have to let it go. I'm still growing as a person, after all. By your silence, you probably think I'm a real jerk for thinking that way about my father. Huh?"

"No, it's not that. It just seems we have—"

All of a sudden a bell rang, which meant class had come to an end. Juan began to open up. "I guess I can identify with you, in a way."

"Why? Is your father a bigger *cabron* than mine?"

The second bell rang. Juan didn't answer Bara's question but replied, "I have to go. See you later, Lieutenant, and thanks for the lesson."

"Where's your salute, soldier?"

"Sorry, sir," apologized Juan.

"Just kidding. Get the hell out of here."

12

As the sunset fell over the mountains and cast a shadow onto the Castle of Chapultepec, the last class was still in session. Professor Tomas was teaching the cadets the mechanics and strategies of battle.

"Now, cadets, to conclude today's lesson, we will finish the review from yesterday's lesson on strategic tactics. Besides physically battling the enemy, in what ways can we engage the enemy? In other words, how can we attack the enemy emotionally?"

"When capturing the enemy, we are to treat them well," Fernando responded.

"Very good. And why would we do that?" Professor Tomas asked.

Fernando added, "Because we could try to help them be more sympathetic to our cause and maybe even have them join our side."

The professor was satisfied with the answer and responded, "Very good, but do you know who came up with that strategy?"

The room was silent. Many cadets began to think about the question, but all came up with blank stares. This amused Professor Tomas, for he knew they probably wouldn't know the answer. So he resumed. "Well, it was Sun Tzu, in his book *Art of War*. Now, I know many of you have not read his book as of yet, but many of his strategies are still applied today. For example, if we replace the enemy's flag with our own, what will this do to our enemy's morale?"

"It demoralizes them; it lets them know they have been conquered," Bara replied.

"Yes. Demoralizing the enemy serves as an indicator that they have been defeated and are completely subdued to the victor. The enemy is under our control. I believe nothing is more depressing than seeing one's flag being taken. So if by chance you see the enemy take your flag, defeat will not be far behind. If you surrender, most likely, you will be able to fight another day."

Bara contemplated asking the following question and decided to ask it. "Sir, is there any shame in surrendering or retreating?"

The professor looked at Bara, pondered for a second, and responded with a delicate tone. "In our lifetime, there will be many things we believe we should be ashamed of. To some, yes, retreating could be one of them. But it shouldn't be, really. One can always live to fight another day. But, in the end, you might not be given a chance to retreat or surrender, and you might have to fight to the death. Leave it to fate or destiny for such an outcome. On a personal note, I would like to believe that I would rather die before I contemplated retreating."

As Fernando heard this, he was curious and asked the professor another question. "Sir, is there any honor in dying? Knowing you fought a losing battle?"

Just as Fernando asked the question, General Monterde entered the classroom. He had been listening to the lecture for a while. The cadets stood up and addressed him. "Good afternoon, General Monterde."

"Good afternoon, cadets. Please sit down. Perhaps, if I may, Professor, I can answer the cadet's question."

Professor Tomas acknowledged General Monterde and let him continue.

"You ask if there is any honor in dying in a losing battle. No, not if you believe what you are fighting for is the just and right thing to do. Now let me ask you a question. Does anyone know the history behind our national flag?"

At first, no one in the room responded. Perhaps it was due to the fact that the class was intimidated by the general's presence. The cadets were second-guessing their thoughts.

So General Monterde began to answer his own question. "According to legend, the gods advised the Aztecs that the place where they should establish their city would be identified when they saw an eagle, perched on a prickly pear tree, devouring a serpent. They saw this mythical eagle on a marshy lake, which is now the main plaza in Mexico City. Does anyone know what the colors on the flag represent?"

The class began to let their guard down and answered the general's question.

"The color red represents the blood that was shed when we fought the Spaniards for independence," Miguel answered.

"That's right. The red represents the blood of our national heroes who gave their lives for freedom—freedom that many saw to be impossible. Many thought it was a losing battle, but if there was a chance, just one chance of making a difference, they would take it."

General Monterde continued. "So we honor those who gave their lives for freedom, which many thought was a losing battle to begin with. Now, what does the white on our flag mean?"

Fernando answered the question with confidence. "The purity of the Catholic faith."

"Very good. And now for the last color, green. In my opinion, it could be viewed as the most important," General Monterde said.

One cadet hesitated with his answer but eventually blurted out, "It means the independence movement. Right, General?"

The general looked at all the cadets and then caught the eyes of young Juan Escutia. "It means so much more than that. It means hope. Hope that we can change as a nation. Hope that one man not only can change his own destiny, but the destiny of a nation."

13

The evening darkness began to creep over the castle, indicating it was time for supper. Many of the Chapultepec staff and cadets were enjoying their supper in the mess hall. Many cadets were talking and laughing. There were soldiers and some cadets in line being served one by one by the cooks. As Vicente and Agustin were about to be served, one cook secretly slipped Vicente a note. Vicente looked at it and then slipped it into his pocket.

Agustin saw the transaction. "What was that?" he asked.

"A note."

"I know that, but from whom?"

"My sister."

"Aren't you going to read it?"

"I'll wait until we get to our dorm room, and why the sudden interest?"

"Well, it must be important if she sent it secretly."

"Maybe, maybe not. You might want to brace yourself for the future, for this is very typical of my sister. She thinks she is a master spy. But this is nothing as to what's in store for you."

"What else is there to know?"

"Oh, you'll find out." Vicente laughed.

"OK, enough about me and your sister. I am just curious about what's written in the note, that's all."

"Just something she wants me to know firsthand that couldn't wait. It might have something to do with Congress or something of that nature."

Agustin's expression was that of curiosity. "And how would she know what goes on in Congress?" he inquired.

"Remember my Aunt Silvia? The one who married the influential official in Mexico City? Well, Aunt Silvia spends a lot of time alone, so she confides in my sister about everything."

"I thought your aunt only attended functions like galas in Mexico City. Your sister says Tia Silvia goes to all of them."

"She does. She also has insomnia, and her husband talks in his sleep. Speaking of my sister, don't forget this weekend is our furlough day."

Agustin's eyes widened with excitement, and he answered, "I am looking forward to it."

"Don't get too excited. Remember, you're still on probation, and I still haven't given you my consent to marry her yet," Vicente warned.

"So you're still a little sore about me courting her?" Agustin said with a smirk.

"After you first told me you liked her, I just couldn't deal with it. You know how protective I am," Vicente said miserably.

"Is that why you attacked me?" Agustin said jokingly.

"I had to kick your ass. You know how hot-tempered I get. I had to get my frustrations out some way," Vicente exclaimed.

"By punching me when I wasn't looking?" Agustin said.

Vicente ignored the last question and answered his previous question. "I needed to see if you were serious about her. When you stood up to me, I knew. I knew then that you were worthy of courting her."

"That and I also had you in a headlock."

Vicente ignored Agustin's statement. "I realized you weren't going to back down, so I gave you a chance to prove yourself and court her. Besides, she could have fallen in love with someone much worse than you, like a *gringo*."

Agustin smiled for a second. "About kicking my ass—who got the worst of that stick?"

"OK, whatever the outcome was, it was for love," Vicente said, changing the direction of the conversation. "Besides, we have to keep the courting a secret. You know there is no socializing or fraternizing while we are still in the academy."

"You need to relax," Agustin reassured Vicente.

"No, what I need from you and her is to be more discreet. And I need her to start acting like the true lady she is."

"You know as well as I do that she does. Besides, you forgive her for everything. She loves you very much. And you also know how headstrong she is."

Vicente put his hands over his head and exclaimed, "Oh, why couldn't God have given me a brother instead?"

"Because he would have looked silly in a dress." As soon as he said this, Agustin leaped from the table and ran out of the cafeteria. Vicente ran right after him. The two cadets laughed as they exited to the castle grounds.

14

First Blood

As a new day began, there was much clamor in the White House; many members were coming and going. Yet it was nothing compared to the House of Representatives. There were many congressmen and senators gathered around in this special joint session called by the president. They were all arguing and yelling at one another. In the midst of the controlled chaos, President Polk sat with a calm demeanor. Eventually, everyone calmed down as the president rose to address the congressmen.

"Gentlemen, please calm down. I only ask this one thing of you."

Congressman Adams rose and addressed the president. "Mr. President, we just want to be clear on what you ask from us."

Adams continued. "And what you just asked is an act of war, sir."

Congressman Lincoln added to the dialogue. "And is this act warranted?"

President Polk stood firm but gave a sympathetic look. "Gentlemen, what happened in south Texas is indeed an act of war on their part. We must respond accordingly."

Congressman Adams was still not convinced of the situation. "So you keep telling us, Mr. President. Could we please hear the report just one more time, for argument's sake?"

Congressman Toombs agreed. "Yes, the full report from General Taylor?"

The vice president stood and read the full report. "Mr. President, the Mexican Army has invaded Texas and ambushed the Thornton scouting party. They have murdered eleven soldiers and captured the rest. A few have escaped. I suppose we can say that hostilities have commenced. In essence, Mexico has invaded our territory and shed American blood upon American soil."

Congressman Lincoln rose. "Mr. President, I do not disagree that a situation has transpired. I just would like to know why Mexico would invade. You continue to say *they* invaded the United States. I would like to know the exact spot where Thornton was attacked and US blood was shed. Mr. President, show me the spot!"

Congressman Lincoln had clearly unsettled the president.

"Remember your place, Congressman. You are a new House member. I would watch my tone, sir."

The president's response was clear and chilling. Congressman Adams came to the aid of Congressman Lincoln. "Mr. Lincoln's youthfulness has no bearing on his question, Mr. President. It is not disrespectful when he asks questions that pertain to the lives of American soldiers. As you know, Mexico has had much turmoil in their country as of late. They would be in no shape to fight at this juncture. We are just trying to speculate if, by chance, they may have been provoked into battle."

President Polk stared at Congressman Adams in a mocking manner. "Congressman Adams, much has changed since you were in office. It is a new world. All we know is we did not provoke them, yet they provoked us."

"Then we shall support General Taylor," Congressman Toombs said.

A second congressman stood and replied, "Yes, and we will send him more troops."

Another congressman rose as well. "We shall take a vote and decide."

President Polk smiled as he prepared to give one of his most heartfelt speeches yet. "Yes, we will. That is the only reason why I have called you all here today. And when you do vote, remember that time is against us. It is why we must act now— to prevent more bloodshed that could fall upon our young men. Have we not learned from what happened at the Alamo? Did we not say it would never happen again to America? This is our chance to prevent a reoccurring act. I am confident in Taylor's expertise and that everything will come full circle. We have a destiny, my fellow Americans. We have God on our side. Manifest Destiny is knocking at our door. And, by God, I intend to answer it."

The vote did not take long, as President Polk had hoped. He reflected that when he had first wanted approval from Congress to go to war, the vote had been sixty-seven Whigs voting against the war. Now, with his final words to Congress, only fourteen congressmen opposed the war. Abraham Lincoln, John Q. Adams, and a few others voted against it. Thus it was decided that the United States would go to war with its neighbor Mexico.

As the men filed out of Congress, Congressman Lincoln attempted to have a word with former President Adams. "Congressman Adams, may I speak with you in confidence?'

"Certainly, son. After today, I feel we both need to express ourselves."

"Sir, this war President Polk wants seems to be warranted out of hatred more than out of policy. I feel President Polk's desire for military glory will be an attractive rainbow that rises after showers of blood."

Congressman Adams smiled. "A bit dramatic, don't you think?"

"I could not help expressing myself, sir. I just think there may be a hidden agenda we are not seeing."

"Well, time will tell, son. Time will tell."

15

Back at the Castle of Chapultepec, many of the cadets were doing their morning chores. Many of these chores were spread out to all the cadets. Some assignments were worse than others. If you asked any of the cadets, the consensus was that cleaning the stables was the worst assignment of them all. Many cadets winced at the thought of cleaning up after the horses, but not Francisco. Just the thought of being around the horses gave him a sense of tranquility because he had grown up with horses back home.

As Francisco began his duties, other cadets were not so concerned with their chores. What Francisco didn't notice was a group of second-year cadets talking among themselves. They seemed to be planning something. After Francisco finished feeding the horses, he began to feed some of the hogs. Off to the other side of the stables were Juan Escutia, Vicente, Fernando, and Bara. They saw these young cadets conspiring and then sneaking up behind Francisco. Suddenly, one of the second-year cadets pushed Francisco head first into the pig trough. Francisco was shocked at first, but then he stood up and began to yell at the cadets. "OK, who pushed me in?"

All the cadets began to laugh, for there was still some pig dung on his head.

"All right, that does it. I'll take every single one of you."

As Francisco said this, he tried to get out of the pig trough and engage the cadets. Since there was so much slop, Francisco slipped as he jumped over the trough and fell to the ground. The cadets were laughing so hard they were crying. Embarrassed, Francisco left the stable to go to his dorm room to get cleaned up. Juan Escutia started to approach the cadets. He was laughing and smiling, as he had witnessed the whole thing. Juan put his arm around the cadets and began talking to them. But Bara had seen enough, and he was not laughing at the incident. Bara began to approach the bullying cadets...

16

In another part of the castle, General Monterde was in his office reading a telegram. When he finished, he put it down, dumfounded by what he had just read. He contemplated his next move. He got up from his chair and walked over to the main door of his office, opened it, and said, "Pedro, please have all the professors come into my office now." Monterde went back to his chair and sat as many of the professors began to enter. Some of the professors were his closest friends. As they all filed in and began to sit down, Monterde blurted out, "The Americans have invaded our country."

General Monterde handed the telegram to the professors. Professor Tomas was the first to respond. "Sir, permission to speak?"

"Go ahead, Tomas. No need to be so formal, not now."

"Sir, didn't the Americans send an envoy to the capital recently to resolve the matter about territory in north Texas?"

General Monterde smiled and answered, "No. Unfortunately, they had other things in mind. They had an agenda to bribe us to sell our country. Land is all they see and want. But this land, this country, is what we fought and bled for. A country of our own."

"How much land do they want, General?"

"Half of Mexico, Tomas."

"But that's preposterous. It will never happen."

"That's what the politicians said to the envoy. As soon as we sent them back to where they came from, a skirmish broke out."

"How big a skirmish, General?" Professor Silva asked.

"Big enough to go to war over. It appears we ambushed a scout troop on our land. They reported we crossed over into their country to do such an act."

"Were there any casualties, General?"

"A total of eleven soldiers were killed, including their commander."

Professor Tomas looked at General Monterde as if there were more to his response. But since there wasn't, Tomas resumed. "And?"

"The rest of the men were taken as prisoners. Some escaped, and the prisoners who were captured were eventually let go."

"General, I hate to sound so callous, but I would assume we would have had to kill at least the whole troop for this to be considered an act of war—if we really wanted to go to war. Besides, we let the prisoners go."

"President Polk knows what he is doing. He is taking full advantage of our situation with the current breakdown of leadership in Mexico. Our army on the border right now doesn't have the leadership it needs to fight. I guess that is why they called Santa Anna to lead the army."

Professor Tomas and the rest of the professors were taken aback. Professor Merced asked, "He's here in Mexico, General?"

"Yes, he entered through the port of Veracruz, and eventually he will go and intercept the Americans in Monterrey."

"And Congress agreed to this?" Professor Tomas interrupted.

"The majority said yes, but there were a few who did not agree with the decision to put him back in command. I would agree that Santa Anna is not the wisest decision, but it seems it's the only one we have for now. I will let the cadets know of the current situation."

"Sir, it seems you have made up your mind, but would that be a wise thing to do, at least for now?"

"If I hesitate in telling them, they will find out one way or another. I will lose their trust, and they will feel that I did not have enough confidence in them to handle the news. I have to tell them, but maybe not everything."

"Is there a chance Santa Anna will be successful?"

"It's too early to tell. Now go and gather the cadets. We need to inform them as soon as possible."

17

All of the cadets were gathered in the mess hall. Many were curious as to why they were meeting at an awkward time. Others were wondering why they were not in class. Francisco was eating an apple and sitting by himself. Suddenly, a second-year cadet approached him. Right behind him were the two others, who had pushed Francisco into the pig trough earlier that day. Francisco saw them approaching and was ready for them, just in case they wanted to fight. They seemed to be approaching him timidly. The first cadet addressed Francisco. "Umm, sorry for what we did. Hope you can forgive us."

"Yeah, it would mean a lot to us if you could forgive us."

Another cadet apologized as well. "Rest assured, it won't happen again. I'm sorry."

The last cadet seemed to be the most remorseful, since he couldn't raise his head. Shocked by this turn of events, Francisco said, "Sure. I guess God wants us to forgive one another, but I will only if you really mean it."

The third cadet replied, "Oh, we do; we do."

As the cadet said this, Francisco noticed he had a huge black eye.

"What happened to your eye?" a curious Francisco asked.

"Well, it's kind of embarrassing. When you left, I laughed so hard that I fell to the ground, and a shovel hit me right on the eye. Dumb luck, I guess. So what do you say? Friends?" the cadet asked nervously.

"Sure. Do you guys want to sit down?" asked Francisco.

"Thanks. No hard feelings?" the cadet asked hopefully.

"Hey, what is done is done," Francisco said optimistically.

"Thanks, Francisco. Hey, is it true your father gave you a Bowie knife?"

"Yeah, he was a…"

As Francisco conversed with the cadets, Bara watched the group from the other side of the hall. It put a smile on his face.

Then General Monterde made his way into the great hall. Many cadets whispered as he entered. The hall suddenly got quiet as the cadets waited for the general to speak. The general began his address. "Gentlemen. Many of you have questions that need answering. Some of you may or may not have heard rumors about the Americans invading Mexico. For now, all that we can tell you is that a skirmish broke out at the border of Texas. This situation will sort itself out. What we need from you is to continue studying and going about your duties. I normally wouldn't be so vague, but I simply don't have all the information for you now. But I will. Rest assured, once I have all the facts, you will have them too. Thank you, gentlemen. Please continue with your assignments."

The cadets dispersed after General Monterde's address. Bara and a few of his friends gathered around the courtyard and began dissecting Monterde's speech.

"What do you think about what the general said?" Bara began.

"I don't know, but it sounded to me like we could all be going home soon," Vicente replied, and he shrugged at the thought.

"Home? Why?" asked Fernando desperately.

"I heard that if the Americans continue to advance, they might not stop at the border. Who knows? They might even make their way to the capital," Vicente said nervously.

"That will never happen. I know there's turmoil at the capital, but I think they would put aside their differences to come together and defeat this aggressor," Bara said with determination.

"But how can we be so sure of that? We need to know what exactly is going on," Fernando replied.

"My sister, she wants to meet me on our furlough day. I will ask her to try to get as much information that she can," Vicente said confidently.

"Good. I, for one, would want to know exactly what we are facing," Bara replied, pleased with the plan.

"What? You don't think the general held back on what he knows?" Fernando asked.

"I think he told us just enough. Besides, he wouldn't want to scare the younger cadets," Bara replied sadly.

"I agree. I don't think they can grasp the magnitude of the situation," Vicente replied.

"Well, it's best if they don't know," Bara said.

"At least for now," Fernando agreed.

Bara looked around. "Shouldn't we have your future brother-in-law in this little gathering?" he jokingly questioned.

"Keep it down, will ya? He is still on probation, in my eyes," Vicente answered, not amused.

Bara said, "What are you waiting for? You trust him enough to court your sister, right?"

"Not only does she gain a husband, but he gets a hot-tempered brother-in-law. What more could a man ask for?" Fernando said.

They all laughed. Vicente stopped smiling and said, "He's had his share of bumps in life—besides the ones I give him. He has a strong character and is a loyal friend. I would be honored if he married my sister. I guess I just like giving him a hard time for my personal amusement."

"You're a sick person, Vicente." Fernando was shocked by Vicente's answer.

"I need to ask you guys something. You know the cadet I've been training—Juan Escutia, right? Do you guys know anything more about him?" Bara said, changing the subject.

"I don't know much about him. He seems like a likeable guy. Besides, I wouldn't give him such a hard time. He seems to always be under Monterde's watchful eye," Vicente answered.

"I've noticed that too. Juan doesn't speak much, though. What is his dorm mate's name again?" Bara asked.

"Francisco, the religious cadet. Oh boy, that kid needs to get some hair on his chest." Vicente smiled as he answered Bara.

"Maybe if he prays real hard, some will grow," Fernando said with a smirk.

They burst into laughter. Bara then noticed that other cadets were gathered at the center of the courtyard.

"Hey, they're doing the mail call. Let's see if we received anything," Bara said as he headed toward the crowd.

The boys were surrounded by the other cadets. They were all in a huddle when young Francisco emerged from the pile. He had a letter. He went to the nearest garden in the castle to be alone and turned around to make sure no one had followed him. He then proceeded to read his letter. Francisco heard his mother's voice as he read his letter.

My dear, beloved son,

How is school? I pray to God that he opens your heart and mind. And what a good heart you have. You make me so proud. I know if your father were alive, he would agree with me. I think of you often, here at the farm. I miss reading you the various passages from the Bible. I also miss seeing your father's smile on you. I am sorry I write to you so much, but you can't blame a mother for loving her only son too much. I just want to know you are in good health. And also to remind you that, if you ever feel alone, take your father's cross and hold it tight. For he and I are always with you. You are a good son. When you are finished with your service, I hope you will become a good soldier as well, a soldier your father would be proud of. I know writing back will be hard in the future while you're in school, but try every once in a while, si? Just let me know you are fine. I miss you very much, and remember to light a candle to the Virgin de Guadalupe. May she watch over you, and please remember to pray our prayer. As the day ends, and though shadows may fall upon my soul, I shall not fear the darkness, but light the world with my love.

18

Trespassing

It was midday, and there was a fire that could be seen on the horizon, as a Mexican town had been taken by American forces. The American army advanced with superior force, and the battle ended as quickly as it had begun. On top of a very large hill stood General Taylor, where he observed everything. This was the first time General Taylor had been to Monterrey, and he wished it were under other circumstances. It was a bittersweet victory for him. Taylor was starting to realize the true reason he and his men were there.

Colonel Clifford made his way to General Taylor. Colonel Clifford wiped smoke from his forehead. The men stared at each other for a second, and both turned to see the effect of their actions. One of their captains approached. As Captain Wilson saluted, he began to speak. "The city and plaza have been taken. What are the general's orders?"

"As of now, I am ordering an eight-week armistice," General Taylor responded.

"A cease-fire, sir?" questioned Captain Wilson.

"Don't you think we have shed enough blood for today, son?" General Taylor inquired.

"Yes, sir. And what about the survivors and prisoners?" asked Captain Wilson.

"Give them *all* safe passage back to their homes."

"Sir?" Captain Wilson quickly realized he had questioned a superior. "Very well, sir," replied the captain as he quickly saluted.

As Captain Wilson left, Taylor faced Colonel Clifford. "What do you think about this war, Colonel?" General Taylor asked, as if searching for some kind of validation.

"I, uh…permission to speak frankly, sir?" replied Clifford, taken aback by the question.

"Please. You are by far the most trustworthy person I can count on, and I need you to be honest with me."

"Thank you, General, for your trust. As for this war, I would like to think that I am doing the right thing, as my father did when he fought the British in 1812 and like the men who fought in the Revolution of Seventy-Six. But this just seems different when I step on this land."

"Those battles were against an aggressor in the United States. They fought for their freedom. Now it seems that *we* could be interpreted as the aggressor."

"That's my point. I don't see or feel the same connection they did when they fought their enemy. But I do believe we have that same tenacity our forefathers had. And we will continue to fight by your side, General Taylor, no matter what the outcome."

A sergeant interrupted General Taylor and Colonel Clifford. "Sir, beg your pardon, General. The captain has his hands full and wants me to give you an update on his progress. We did as you requested. We let those savages go back to their homes."

General Taylor gave the young sergeant a stern look and with a menacing tone replied, "Son, if you describe the enemy with such disdain again, you will be scrubbing pans until rust grows from your fingertips. Do I make myself clear?"

The young sergeant looked as if he had wet his pants. "Understood, sir. Sorry, sir. Please excuse me, sir."

"Dismissed, soldier. You know, John, men like this, and these volunteers, will be the death of me," General Taylor commented.

"They just need more discipline, sir."

"I guess you're right. I want you to take some scouting parties into the surrounding towns. There are three in particular: Tres Rios, Junta Verde, and Agua Nueva. I want you to retrieve food and supplies at Agua Nueva."

"Yes, sir, General."

"And Colonel, do you believe President Polk when he says we have a divine right to be here?" General Taylor caught himself and retracted his question. "Don't answer that. Dismissed, Colonel."

"Very well, General."

As Taylor watched, the colonel disappeared from sight. "I am beginning to see there is nothing divine about this war," Taylor murmured as he answered his own question.

19

As days passed, the American army continued its advance toward the capital. Many Mexican citizens, as well as the government, did not believe the American army would, or could, cross into the heart of Mexico City. They believed Santa Anna would be able to crush the American forces that threatened Mexican sovereignty. The local townspeople continued to go on with their lives. Vendors in the marketplace commenced their morning setup. This huge attraction brought many people.

Even cadets Vicente and Agustin were admiring the sights. As the two were talking and laughing, they suddenly saw Vicente's sister, Merced. As they approached each other, Vicente embraced his sister. And she gave Agustin a loving smile. Agustin got flustered when he saw Merced. When Vicente and Merced broke their embrace, Agustin gave Merced a polite greeting, very formal since they were in the public eye.

"Did you get my message?" Merced began informing her brother of the latest news.

Vicente rolled his eyes and replied, "Next time, just send it by mail."

"Well, with the current crisis in Texas, I thought you would want to know as soon as possible. And considering what I have to tell you, I thought it best this way."

"What has happened?" Vicente was now more curious than ever.

"Apparently, a few weeks ago, an American envoy came to the capital and offered Mexico an extreme amount of money."

"In exchange for what?" asked Agustin.

"Mexico."

"What did the politicians do?" Vicente asked.

"They sent the envoy on their way with a reply of never, which could explain the reason for the attack on the border and their movement into Mexican territory."

"Good, but now what?" Agustin asked.

"Now we wait," Merced replied.

"Is that everything?" Vicente asked.

"For now, yes."

"Very well. Once we get back, we have to tell…"

Vicente stopped midsentence and fixed his eyes upon a vision. He saw an attractive young lady across the marketplace. The young lady had gotten her dress caught on a table of one of the vendors. Without missing a beat, Vicente said to Merced and Agustin, "Well, if you'll excuse me, it is time for me to be a hero. And please remember what I said about being discreet, both of you."

Vicente leaped toward the young lady and assisted her by unhooking her dress in an instant. He introduced himself. Both Merced and Agustin saw this and could only imagine what they were talking about. Agustin then turned his attention to Merced. "Miss Suarez, would you like to go for a walk?"

"Why, I would love to."

"Nice weather we are having; do you not agree?"

"Yes, it is," Merced answered, and then she changed the subject. "How's the academy?"

"So far, it's great. It's just hard concentrating when I think of you all the time," Agustin replied.

"I do sometimes think about you," Merced replied with coyness.

"I have missed you a lot. And when you are not around, I can't think straight."

Merced blushed and tried to change the subject again. "Back to school. Are the classes getting harder?"

"Well, some are, but your brother is a good friend and tutor. We help each other out."

"That sounds helpful. Our parents demand a lot of him."

"I bet." Merced noticed that Agustin got a little sullen at the mention of her parents.

"Oh, I'm sorry. I am proud of you as well."

"Thank you, but it is all right. It has been a long time since I lost my family. Well, you know that already. But you have been my family, since we were just kids. What I remember most is the way you took care of me that night of the storm, remember?"

"How could I forget? You got soaked putting all the horses back into the stables, and you got a fever."

"And after that, how you took care of me." Agustin smiled at Merced.

"I was just being a good Catholic." Merced smiled back.

"A good Catholic, huh? Is that why you stood by my bedside for days?"

"Of course." Merced blushed.

"And brought me fresh flowers?"

"Well, I thought the smell of the flowers might bring you some comfort." Merced smiled once again.

"The same flowers that you love growing in your garden. Roses, right? They did bring me comfort. When the fever hit me the most, the flowers were one of the two things that made me feel at peace."

"What was the other?" Merced asked curiously.

"You." Agustin then faced Merced with the most loving stare and said, "That was when I knew I loved you more than anything. It's funny, but when I close my eyes, I can still smell those roses."

"You can?" Merced got all choked up.

"And I also see your face," Agustin said, smiling. "And that is a sight I always want to see."

Agustin then drew Merced closer and pulled out a small ring from his pocket. He gently took her hands and noticed she was speechless. He broke the silence by saying, "I know I want to spend the rest of my life with you, and when the time comes, we will be married. Many may think we are too young to be in love. That is why I want you to wait for me."

"As long as it takes, I will be here for you. I love you," Merced said as she looked at Agustin with watery eyes.

Agustin could not control his emotions. He pulled Merced into a warm embrace, and, as he kissed her, he forgot all that was around him. He didn't even notice Vicente running toward them.

At first, Vicente was shocked to see his sister and Agustin embrace, but then he realized why he was running to them in the first place.

"You call this discreet? We have to go now!"

"What's wrong?" Agustin asked.

"They're calling all the cadets back to the castle. Sorry, Merced, but we have to go."

"Is everything all right?" Merced asked nervously.

"We just got word the Americans have attacked Monterrey," Vicente said, almost with disbelief. "I will write to you—promise. But, for now, we have to go."

Merced was shocked by the news and was silent. She looked frightened, but Agustin gave her some comfort by saying, "It will be all right, Merced."

Merced nodded and added, "You will write to me as well, though, won't you?"

"Of course I will. Don't worry," Agustin said.

"I love you both," Merced said.

She hugged her brother and whispered in his ear. "Please take care of Agustin."

"I will," Vicente whispered back.

As they began to leave, Agustin turned back and saw anguish upon Merced's face. He wanted to console her but could not come up with anything. As the cadets headed back to the castle and were far enough away from Merced, Vicente grabbed Agustin by the arm and addressed him. "Oh, yeah. I forgot one thing."

"What is it?"

"This."

Vicente punched Agustin right on the mouth. Agustin fell to the ground and looked up at Vicente, startled.

"That's for kissing my sister and not being discreet about it. Now I've got to watch out for your ass." Vicente groaned.

"Well, I hope you treat your brother-in-law better than this in the future, since Merced agreed to marry me," Agustin responded as he rubbed his chin while he stayed on the ground.

"Ha ha, very funny." Vicente noticed that Agustin was not laughing.

"What do you mean?" Vicente asked Agustin in a combative stance.

Agustin braced himself for another impact. "I mean I proposed to your sister, and she said yes. That is why I was kissing her!" he declared. Waiting to exchange blows with Vicente, Agustin began to notice Vicente was trembling.

"Why, that has got to be one of the most craz...stup...insan...most wonderful things you have ever done. You are going to make my sister the happiest she has ever been, or we're going to have a problem."

Vicente looked at Agustin and then stretched his hand out to help Agustin get up. As soon as he did, Agustin replied, "I will." Agustin hesitated for a second and added, "I promise. Now let's get back."

The boys looked at each other and continued to run to the castle, laughing.

20

Tension was brewing at the White House. The staff felt it all around the grounds. It was mostly due to President Polk's obsession and the unusual amount of time he spent in the war room. The president insisted that every decision and every step be made by him. Many were under the assumption he had been planning this war for a long time. There were men all around him debating what the next move should be. Suddenly, they were interrupted by a messenger. All stopped talking, ready to hear updated news.

"Mr. President, a telegram from General Taylor." The messenger handed him the telegram. Polk's worried face instantly turned into a smile as he read the telegram.

He began to read the news aloud to his delegates. "It is with great pride I inform you General Taylor has defeated the Mexicans in Monterrey and has taken their Independence Hill."

The men cheered when they heard the news. Polk continued reading. "This has to be one of our finest victories yet. General Taylor has also agreed to…"

Polk began to read the telegram silently. His smile was slowly fading. He then yelled at the men around him. "Out. All of you, out," Polk shouted, but he suddenly caught himself and calmed down. "Gentlemen, please give me a moment with my generals and the vice president."

The rest of the men left the office, confused. Polk then addressed the generals. "That ignorant hick," Polk stated.

"Sir, what happened? Did General Taylor not say he secured the victory in Monterrey?" the vice president respectfully asked.

"Yes," Polk replied, and started to laugh as he continued to read the telegram. "But he also agreed to an eight-week armistice, and he has allowed the Mexican forces to retreat peacefully back to their homes. Taylor should have crushed them all at once. Instead, he let those Mexicans live to fight another day."

"But, Mr. President, General Taylor is just applying what seems fit—a code of ethics, so to speak. He is being respectful to his enemy. By all accounts, he is being humane."

"Humane? Humane? That shall be his undoing. I assumed he understood what I...I mean what we thought best for the United States. But you are right; General Taylor is being too humane."

Polk pondered his next remark. He was recalibrating his strategy. "And that is something I cannot have." Polk gave an order to one of his generals. "Have General Taylor hold a defensive position at his current location and not pursue any further offensive action with his troops. I am changing his command as of now. I need someone to follow my orders without hesitation."

Polk continued to give his orders with a sense of a preda-
tory strategy. "Have General Scott ready to deploy. He shall assume command. And give him two-thirds of Generals Taylor's
army. Make sure the soldiers we give Scott have combat experience. Leave Taylor with the volunteers."

"General Scott, Mr. President?" Vice President Dallas
asked so carefully.

"Scott is a good soldier who follows orders. That is a trait
lacking in this room. General Scott will lead my army to
victory."

General Smith responded with a gentle demeanor, "Mr.
President, to have General Taylor withdraw his forces—do
you think this will sit well with him?"

"The general will do as he is told. I have given him an order, and he will follow it to the letter. Now let us focus on our
plans with Scott. Please have the rest of the men come back
into my office, and make the necessary arrangements for a
full deployment on the shores of Veracruz."

21

Moral Dilemma

Several months had passed, and the American forces had now penetrated several key entries into Mexico. As the American navy was attempting to make its final push toward Mexico City, a fleet of ships was at the Gulf of Mexico with one more stronghold left for them to demolish: the Port of Veracruz. As American forces sailed toward the shorelines of Veracruz, one could see all the American faces on the ships. In the midst of the soldiers, Colonel Clifford always seemed to stand out. Clifford had earned the respect of every man onboard. John Clifford had entered West Point Academy when he was nineteen years old. In the last few years, he had seen many battles, and his expertise on strategic warfare was flawless. He had been recognized by General Taylor and President Polk for his bravery in the assault on Saltillo. Clifford was frustrated with his current actions in the war and was worried that someone might notice.

"As the Mexican Army continues to fight with such passion, why do I identify with them so much? These Mexicans are dying for their country—the same sacrifice I would make for my own. Is their sacrifice any less than mine?" Clifford began to ponder.

For the moment, Clifford wanted to be lost in the wind as it blew through his hair. He smiled as the cool breeze rushed across his face. Clifford imagined being in a different time and place and did not notice General Scott approaching.

General Scott disrupted Clifford's moment of peace. "May I have a word with you, Colonel?"

"But of course, General. Whatever can I do you for?" a startled John responded.

"Clifford, I have noticed a sense of disagreement in your manner."

"Sir?"

"Help me understand. General Taylor holds you in the highest regard and has recommended you for various commendations, yet you requested to be transferred out of his unit. I also have heard from numerous sources you are still bothered by what happened in Agua Nueva. Is there a connection, Colonel?"

"What happened in Agua Nueva is something I would soon like to forget, General."

"I need to know all my men are at their full capacity mentally when confronting the enemy, sir. Please go on."

"You do know what happened in Agua Nueva? I mean from the report. Right, General?"

"I have read it, as well as heard various rumors. My impression of the incident is that some men were relieving some of their stress with the local townspeople."

The general smiled as he said this. Clifford noticed it and in a monotone voice responded, "Stress, General? It was far more than stress. It was needless killing. When we finished overtaking the town of Agua Nueva, a group of scouts and I investigated a cave near the town to see if there were any Mexican soldiers hiding in it. That was when we heard the screams. At first, I thought we were going to be attacked. But it was the yelling of women and children. These so-called volunteers in our army dragged twenty families into that cave, and that was when the slaughter began. They started with the men. When we arrived, we saw the men dead in pools of blood. Then we saw the women and children clinging onto the legs of those murderers, begging for their lives. All they wanted was mercy; all they got was a bayonet to the stomach."

"Then what happened?" General Scott asked, not shocked by what he was hearing.

"I gave a command, and we took aim on the volunteers who were preying on the defenseless Mexicans and forced them out. All 109 soldiers filed out cursing us like wild, rabid dogs. I was a hairpin close to giving the order to shoot. But I thought General Taylor should be the one to give such an order."

"So you wanted to discipline the volunteers."

"Discipline? No, sir, I wanted to punish them. Those volunteers deserved to get what they inflicted."

"But you know full well that would not have been prudent."

"Yes, sir. General Taylor told me he could not afford to lose a hundred men."

"Clearly not a hundred, nor one of your men in the midst of battle. I have met Taylor. I was not, in the least, impressed by the man. But I do agree with his decision pertaining to those soldiers. If Taylor would have punished those 'volunteers,' that message would have caused disdain for the rest of the army."

"I wanted justice to be done, sir," Clifford said desperately.

"We are at war, Colonel. There will be many incidents we don't approve of, but we cannot afford to demoralize our troops."

"But, sir, what they did to those women and children, not to mention the destruction of the town—it goes against everything I believe in, sir."

"That is, unfortunately, the cost of war," Scott replied smugly.

"The cost, sir?" Clifford responded with disbelief. Clifford realized he was beginning to raise his voice and decided to continue at a normal tone. "At what cost, begging your pardon? I would do anything for my country. I have proven that, with duty and honor. But when I see the Mexican people die for theirs, it makes me question whether we are here for the right reason."

"Right or wrong, we are here for the duration of this war. We will be victorious. We are doing God's will, and our actions will be viewed as such by our sons and by their sons. History will declare we did the right thing. But for now, we have orders. And those orders must be obeyed. Many more men will die; that is clear. We just have to make sure it's more of them than us."

22

A s night fell upon the Castle of Chapultepec, so did the tension of many cadets. They heard the news of the American army invading various parts of Mexico, and rumors emerged that they could make their way into the heart of Mexico. This propelled the young cadets into a state of anxiety. Many tried to continue carrying out everyday duties and chores. One of the duties was to maintain a watchful eye on the castle. Older cadets patrolled the castle and eventually found themselves talking to one another to keep themselves awake and not focus on the threat that was making its way up to them. Most of the cadets were supposed to be in bed. The patrolling cadets disengaged from their conversations and continued to patrol the castle.

Suddenly, two cadets appeared, sneaking in the shadows. They were creeping from one entrance to an exit leading into the forest. The cadets wore civilian clothing. The silence was broken when Agustin questioned his friend Vicente. "Where exactly are we going?"

"Quiet. We are going to the center of the forest. Now, remember, if we get caught, our hides are worth shit. Merced has some news for us," Vicente said anxiously.

"Sorry, just got impatient. Well, anyway, what's so important that we have to meet her at midnight?" Agustin whispered.

"She couldn't tell me, but believe me, it's well worth it. I think. Trust me, OK? And don't make me regret telling you."

"Fine, sorry."

When the boys approached the end of the exit, they noticed a large metal lock. A prepared Vicente had the key to open it. They entered a tunnel that led them into the forest. It was a secret tunnel only a few cadets knew about.

"How did you know about this tunnel?" Agustin asked.

"Bara told me once. When he first learned he wouldn't be transferred, he almost ran off. But sense got the better of him, and he stayed at the castle."

"And he just told you of this place?"

"Well, we were drinking tequila one night, and he blurted it out."

"So I guess we have to thank tequila for his secret." Agustin smirked.

"I guess so. We are close to where we need to be."

As the boys exited the tunnel, they saw a dim light in the distance. Vicente pulled out a lantern that he had concealed from Agustin. As he lit the lantern, he put his hand in front of it and waited. He saw the dim light go off. Vicente then waved his hand up and down in front of the lantern. The dim light reappeared and then was extinguished.

"What happened?" asked Agustin.

"Nothing. We just wait," Vicente replied as he extinguished his light as well.

The boys heard a movement in the forest that began to approach them. As a slender figure appeared before them, its shape began to light up with the moonlight, and Vicente's sister appeared clearly. Vicente embraced her and spoke. "I read your note. You seemed upset."

"Sorry, it's just that what I have to tell you is very important," Merced said desperately.

"It must be if we are risking our service meeting you here! I mean, I am glad to see you, but this is a great risk," Vicente replied restlessly.

"The Americans have invaded. They conquered Veracruz and are now advancing to the capital."

Vicente was in shock by the news. "Then that means—"

"Only one thing," Agustin interrupted, realizing the gravity of the situation.

"They are coming straight toward us because we are on the way to the capital," a saddened Vicente replied.

"Yes," Merced answered quietly. She resumed. "They say Santa Anna will save us. That he will intercept them and crush them. He even had a chance to do it in Monterrey against Taylor's army."

"What happened?" Agustin inquired.

"Santa Anna was called back to the capital because a mini revolution was breaking out. General Santa Anna had Taylor on the run but decided to concede. He left when he got news from the capital."

"To just leave—that doesn't make sense," Vicente said.

Merced looked at her brother as she explained. "It does if your interests are in jeopardy; the politicians are the ones who are paying for your service and protection."

Vicente thought for a second and said, "I guess, but why did you call us here tonight? We would have gotten the news eventually."

"I am leaving the city. Word is the Americans are threatening many villages along the way, and our mother wants me to travel north with her to California as a precaution. She says we are not safe here anymore," Merced replied unhappily.

"You're leaving?" Vicente was shocked by the news.

"I have to," Merced exclaimed. "But I also wanted to persuade you both to come with me."

"Do you know what you're asking?" Vicente said aggressively.

"I know, I know, but I have a feeling this might be the last time I see either one of you," a frustrated Merced said.

Vicente answered with a prideful tone, "Duty and honor above all else. That's what father taught me before I joined the academy. After he had his stroke and lost all mobility, I vowed I would be his hands and feet and carry out his wishes of being a great soldier like him. So you know my answer."

Vicente then turned to Agustin. He hesitated for a second and said, "But I cannot answer for Agustin."

Agustin looked at Merced and then at Vicente, then back to Merced. "I...I really want to, but..." Agustin said. He couldn't come up with the right words to express himself.

Vicente broke the silence. "If it's my blessing you want, my blessing you'll have."

Merced got tearful and then leaned toward her brother and hugged him. "Oh, thank you, *hermanito*. I love you so much."

She went toward Agustin, and he answered with a feeling of gratitude. "It means a lot to me that you have given me her hand in marriage—"

"So we will leave tonight. I have the horses waiting for us—" Merced interrupted.

"But because I love you so much, I cannot go with you," Agustin replied.

Vicente was trying to comprehend the situation. "I gave you my consent already, and you don't have to worry about the general. I will figure something out."

"It's not that," Agustin said in frustration.

"Well, what is it? Is it that you don't want to marry me?" Merced was trying to comprehend Agustin's reply.

Agustin looked at Merced earnestly and said, "More than anything else in the world, my love, but if the Americans attack, I…I have to stay and defend the castle. It's not only something I have to do, it's something I need to do."

Merced began to weep and embraced Agustin. As they embraced each other, Merced wiped away her tears on Agustin's shoulder.

"But I don't want to lose you," Merced answered.

Vicente, standing in the midst of an awkward situation, said, "I will leave you two alone, for the sun will be rising soon, and you'll have to make your choice."

Merced embraced her brother for the last time. "I love you. May God protect you. I will tell Father how his brave son stayed and fought the enemy."

"Thanks, *hermanita*, but try to persuade him to go with you. He is a good soldier, so I think he will make a good husband. I will always have you in my heart." Vicente then faced Agustin and said, "Whatever decision you make, I will support you. I chose my path; now choose yours. Good luck."

Vicente left them both and headed back into the tunnel. Merced and Agustin were alone.

"Isn't there anything I can say or do to persuade you to come with me?"

Agustin pulled Merced into his arms. "I am sorry, my love, but no." Agustin looked into Merced's eyes and said, "Merced, nothing will happen to me, I promise."

"I can't live with the thought of losing you," Merced said tearfully.

"You won't lose me. Not now, not ever. Merced, we'll never be apart. Not in this lifetime. No matter what, I will be with you always. I promise."

"Then why don't you leave with me? Tonight."

"If I leave now, then the Americans will have already won. They expect us to feel afraid, scared that we can't protect ourselves. I realize I am not staying here for me, but for all those who gave their lives to protect us. I want you, me, and our future children to live in a free Mexico, without fear."

"I'm sorry for being selfish," Merced said. She tried to compose herself but failed miserably.

"You're not selfish. It gives me great joy to know you love me so much that you want to be with me. But I will always be with you; you have a piece of me that will always live on. Nothing will happen to me. We will be together."

"You keep saying that, but how do you know?" Merced asked hopefully.

"Oh, darling, don't you know by now? Death could claim me in battle and engulf me in darkness, but the flame of our love will light my way to you—always to you," Agustin said passionately.

"I love you, Agustin. I will always remember this moment."

They embraced and kissed with such purity that Agustin shed a tear. Agustin looked at his future bride but said nothing. He gazed into Merced's eyes and started to leave, hiding his face as tears began to fall down his cheeks. He stood still, with his back to Merced.

"And I too will always remember this moment. Remember the roses you grew in your garden? When this blasted war is over, I will give you a huge garden so that you can have fresh flowers everyday. Roses are your favorite flower, right?" Agustin declared.

"Yes," Merced said, weeping.

"I always knew roses were your favorite. I could close my eyes and smell a rose fragrance on you like sweet perfume. If you close your eyes, I bet you could smell them right now." Agustin then turned and faced Merced. "Close your eyes and imagine your garden now, and think about your roses. Can you smell them? Can you? Close your eyes and imagine all the flowers in your garden," he said.

Merced closed her eyes and imagined her garden. She concentrated for a few seconds more and said, "I can smell them. I smell them, Agustin. I smell the flowers and the roses. The smell is so pretty, I..." she said with a smile. And when she opened her eyes, Agustin was nowhere in sight. Merced realized he had wanted to leave her with a beautiful image.

She fell to her knees and began to pray. "Oh, dear God, protect them both with your mercy. I beg of you."

Merced wept through the night.

23

Inconvenient Truth

A few days passed as rumors furiously flew through the halls of the Castle of Chapultepec. A sullen mood fell upon the castle. There had not been any new news given to the students about the American army approaching the castle. The general wanted the cadets to focus on their studies and not the threat approaching them. The only news the general had was that the Americans had obliterated and conquered the Port of Veracruz. He also heard that the Americans had attacked Santa Anna in Monterrey and that Santa Anna had retreated from battle. As the Americans were getting closer to Churubusco, the general realized the American army would soon be on their doorstep. Not belittling the situation, Monterde believed this was not the type of news he wanted to relay to the cadets, at least for now. So the general decided to distract the cadets and brighten up the mood in the castle. He made an announcement to gather all the cadets later in the day. When the general had all the cadets assembled in the courtyard, he addressed them.

"Men, it has been a while since we have had a furlough day. I would like for us to have a bonfire. Tonight, there will be no rank between us. We will all commune as one, just as Mexican citizens. There will be no curfew tonight. You have the night to ride horses and stay up to talk with your fellow cadets and teachers. You can write to loved ones if you wish, but, in the end, try to make the most of your time. I am proud of the way you have all handled our current situation. You have demonstrated great inner strength under these trying times. That said, you are dismissed."

Later that night, all the cadets were running about the castle. Some of the cadets were in the stables caring for their horses. Others were in their rooms writing. A small group of cadets had gathered around the bonfire and were staring into the light. Many didn't know what to say.

Bara stood up and addressed his friends. "Well, we don't know what the future holds for each of us. I just know we will all face it together. Many of my friends have made me a better friend, and I hope I have helped you become better soldiers at the same time. So I just want to say thank you, and it has been an honor to serve with you all."

"You're welcome," Fernando replied.

"Very funny, but in all seriousness, you are the best friends and band of cadets I have had the honor to serve with."

Fernando, who was usually reserved, made an impromptu speech. "I cannot believe I am going to do this. But, since we are laying everything on the table, I just want to get something off my chest." He paused. "I found something that I thought I had lost a long time ago, when I lost my parents."

"And what was that?" Bara replied, intrigued.

"A family. I haven't told too many people exactly how my parents died. In fact, I have only told one person, and even he does not know the whole story. But since I am among family, I guess I can share with you all. When my father was in the military, he lost an arm in a demonstration," Francisco began.

"How?" Fernando asked.

"He was instructing his platoon on how to strategically fire a cannon. A soldier did not pay attention and put too much powder in the cannon. When they fired the cannon, my father got the worst of it. After that, the military really had no more use for him. They considered him half a soldier. His spirit was broken for a while. Then he decided to retire and move to a small pueblo close to Sierra Madre. The town had no real order, and it was in need of law and order. The town heard of my father's record and offered him a job as the local authority. It made my father very happy, and he became as he had once been, before the accident. He was a proud man. He never backed down to anyone. But he did not know about some local bandits, known as the Diablos, who would raid the town every now and then."

Bara was dumbfounded, since he had never heard this story.

"Los Diablos?" Bara asked.

"Yes, they murdered my parents," Fernando said sadly.

"How? I mean, if you don't mind my asking?" Bara asked without thinking.

"Even though it all happened so fast, I will never forget what they did, nor forget their faces. Their leader, he had a scar across his face and had one arm as well. My mother and I were hiding when they came to our house. But when I had the chance, I peeked out through a cracked window and could see what was happening outside. The one-armed bandit challenged my father one-on-one. My father never backed down, nor feared death. He thought it was going to be a fair fight, as he only saw his challenger. Little did my father know, that the one-armed man had his gang hiding on both sides of the house. As soon as my father drew his weapon, the whole gang shot him with an array of bullets. When the firing finished, the leader walked over to my father.

"'Did you really think I would jeopardize my leadership like that? You must be really stupid,' the leader said, laughing."

Fernando scoffed in disbelief as he continued. "So much for honor, but what was amazing was that he was still alive. Their leader went up to my father, and as my father lay there dying, he begged for my and my mother's safety. Their leader then cocked his gun and shot my father right between his eyes."

"What happened next?" Francisco asked.

"My mother screamed and hid me in my father's foot trunk. As soon as they heard the scream, they rushed into the house. My mother grabbed one of my father's rifles and started shooting. She probably thought she would spook them away. But they just rushed in and shot her where she stood. I heard them come closer. I was so scared. I thought, what would my father do? He would have faced his fear, no matter the consequences. But I did nothing. I just froze, right in the trunk, paralyzed with fear."

"Did they find you?" Bara tried to empathize with Fernando.

"No, they started taking what they could until they heard shots being fired outside the house. The gang then ran out to see who was shooting. It turned out, the townspeople had gotten together and formed a posse. The Diablos then got on their horses and rode away.

"Since then, I vowed to push myself and face my fears. To avenge his death, I dedicated myself to becoming one of the most skillful soldiers I could be, so that I could use what I had learned to track them down. But when I applied to this school, General Monterde helped turn my hate into something more productive. He made me realize that I needed to choose my own path. That it could be a path of hate or a path of peace. So I chose peace. I'm glad I did because I get to share that peace with my friends, who have become my family."

"Just when I thought I knew someone. I know it took a lot of guts for you to tell us that. And, as a family, we will always be by your side," Bara responded.

"Well, since you are my family, I have no reason to keep any secrets from any of you," Fernando said.

When Juan Escutia heard this, he crumbled inside a little.

Bara directed his attention to the rest of the cadets. "Well, since we are all sharing, does anyone else have something to say?"

One by one, the cadets started to share with one another. Juan slowly left the group. He found himself walking along the halls all alone. Francisco saw him from afar. As Juan continued to walk away, Francisco noticed the cadets who had pushed him into the pig trough avoid Juan like the plague, as if they were afraid of him. Francisco was curious as to the reason, so he decided to approach Bara, since Bara seemed to know everything that went on around the castle. Once Francisco got closer to Bara, he whispered, "Bara, can I talk to you for a moment?"

"Sure. Do you need something?"

"Hum, not really, just curious. I just wanted to ask you something. You saw what happened to me at the stables a while ago, right?"

Bara seemed surprised that Francisco would bring up the embarrassing incident. "Yeah, I remember. I just thought you might want to forget it."

"Do you know how James got his black eye?"

"Well, it's weird how it happened. Strange, really."

"Strange? In what way?"

"Well, after what happened to you, I was about to go up to them and reprimand them. But Fernando stopped me when he saw Juan approaching them."

"What happened?" Francisco was even more curious.

"Well, Juan was laughing so hard at the incident that I thought he was applauding them for such a stunt. When he approached the cadets, Juan patted them on the back like old chums. Then, all of a sudden, he struck Cadet James right in the eye."

"Juan punched them?" Francisco said, incredulous.

"No, just James. And, by the way he did it, the other cadets got scared right away. Juan picked him up and whispered something in his ear. Then Juan just walked away."

"What happened next?" Francisco inquired, as if he were listening to a bedtime story.

"Cadet James whispered something to the other cadets. They all got really serious and left. I was taken aback at first, then I never thought about it again."

"Why would Juan do that?" Francisco asked himself out loud.

"That's something you would have to ask him."

Francisco, absorbed by what he had just heard, went to his dorm room.

24

Meanwhile, Juan made his way to the general's office. As he entered the dark main office, he saw a light piercing underneath General Monterde's office door. Juan saw a movement underneath the door. He held his breath and knocked.

"Yes?" General Monterde answered.

"Sir, it's me, Cadet Escutia. May I come in to have a word with you?"

There was a long pause.

"One moment. I, um…certainly, son, come on in."

Juan slowly entered the office and saw the general sitting in his chair with glasses sliding down his nose. In front of him was a small set of figurines. They appeared to be small metal soldiers. As Juan continued to look around, he noticed there were several small soldiers throughout the office. The general's desk seemed like a glorified craft station.

"Thank you, sir!" Juan said graciously.

"It seems like you caught me in one of my few pleasures."

"What were you doing, sir, if I may ask?" Juan asked cautiously.

"I like to keep my hands busy. When I was younger, I would collect tin gunpowder flasks. The flasks were left behind by soldiers. My father and I would pound the tin until it was flexible and thin enough. We would make small figurines. It was a simple hobby that I shared with my father. He made a little bit of money selling them, but it was really a way for us to bond. The ones you see before you are my little tin soldiers; they represent the soldiers who fought in our Battle of Independence and other historic battles."

Juan was about to pick one up, not knowing how truly fragile they were. The general stopped him. "Careful, Juan. They are fragile. I mean, they bend easily," Monterde said.

"Sorry, sir," Juan said.

"It's quite all right. Please, go ahead and pick one up. Just be careful," Monterde said forgivingly.

Juan picked one up.

"The one you have is General Anaya. He may seem small, but he was a great soldier." Monterde smiled and added, "Many, if not all, of these soldiers were brave. Men who gave their lives for their beliefs and for independence."

"Small but tough—like us, huh, sir?" Juan said, as if he wanted approval.

"You could say that. Well, enough of my hobbies. What can I do for you? It's getting quite late," Monterde said.

"Sir, you have always been forthright with me," Juan said as he laid the small figure back down.

"And I always will. What is your question?" Monterde asked skeptically.

"Were the Diablos responsible for the deaths of Fernando's parents?"

Monterde was shocked by the question. "Why...I mean, how did you..." He stared into Juan's eyes. "Yes, from what I know, they were," Monterde responded as if his heart were sinking a little bit.

"It makes me sick to my stomach to think about what happened. But did you know it was *he* who took the final shot that killed Fernando's father?" Juan probed Monterde, his eyes full of anger toward his father.

"If you are asking me if your father was the one who took the final shot, I do not know," Monterde answered honestly.

"Sir, Fernando told us everything." Juan was now more puzzled than ever.

"All I know is that the Diablos were responsible, but I did not know for sure that your father was the one responsible for ending his father's life," Monterde said.

"Sir, could you please tell me everything about my father? Not just that he was with the Diablos. I want to know everything, and please don't hold back."

"It's getting late, and it's too long a story." Monterde knew the truth would be too much to bear for anyone.

"Sir...please."

Monterde saw the anguish in Juan's eyes. "Very well. Your father and I served together. We were the best of friends, you might say. Well, when the war was over, he could not adjust to civilian life. It seemed he wanted to continue to wage war on everything and anyone. For ten years, he traveled all across the world to look for war to satisfy his appetite for destruction. He unleashed so much rage; he had no other choice but to come back home, for he was a wanted man. He was different from the man I had once known. Then he did something so unexpected. He married a beautiful woman named Rosa. He then had a son. I thought he was a changed man.

"Soon after, he invited me to visit him, to see his child. I believed that to be the reason, but that was not the case. When I went to see him, he obviously had had too many shots of tequila, for he was very drunk. He was happy to see me. He started to explain that he had a plan to take advantage of the current crisis in the capital and wanted to get a group of ex-soldiers to ravage the countryside. He wanted me to join his troop. I declined. He was annoyed with my decision. He said I was dead to him and asked me to leave.

"I heard a commotion in the house when I was preparing my horse. I heard him arguing with his wife. I could hear her telling him that he could leave right then and there, but he could not take their child. Then I heard a gunshot. As I ran back into the house, I saw she was shot. He said it was an accident. I checked on her and confirmed she was dead. I took his child. I told him he could leave, but he would have to leave his child—*you*. The child would not live a life of evil like his father.

"He got furious and started shooting at me. He missed, since he was too drunk to shoot straight. I shot him in the arm. It wasn't a mortal wound. He fell, head first, straight onto a tequila bottle, and it cut his face pretty bad. I didn't know my shot had done the most damage; I heard he lost his arm. Since then, he has never tried to see you, nor has he confronted me again. I took you in and forged papers to have you assigned to different schools. I changed your name as well. Then you came to this institution, and I told you who your father was, that you needed to know he was associated with the gang, the Diablos, but that was all I told you."

A sorrowful Monterde waited for Juan's response.

"Now I know the whole truth about him," Juan said, saddened by Monterde's story.

"So the question now is, what will you do with the knowledge that your father killed Fernando's father?" The general paused and resumed trying to comfort Juan. "I know that this will not be any consolation, but it brought me great joy to have you here at the academy, even though I could not get close to you. It would not have sat well with the other cadets. They could have targeted you as my favorite. I was afraid—afraid they would have seen right though me. Afraid they would have seen the love one has for a child, a son. So I kept my distance from you because I did not want your life to be any harder than it already was." Monterde's voice cracked as he responded compassionately.

"Thank you, sir. Your words mean a lot. I know it must have been difficult for you all these years. And you have no idea how I really appreciate your candor and honesty. But I still can't avoid it, can I? The blood my father shed has followed me every step of the way—to this castle, my school, my home. Now he has tarnished everything good that has happened to me. I wish I had that hope you once told me about. You know, changing one's destiny. But it just seems so hopeless now."

"Son, you cannot live like that. I will tell you what I told Fernando. You can't let hate, fear, or guilt rule your life. You have the choice to follow the path you want," Monterde said.

"What happens if there are no paths left open for me? Just the one my father left me? I thank you, sir, for everything. I will see myself out."

Juan left the general's office sadly. Monterde stood up and watched Juan leave. He made a motion to suggest he wanted Juan to stay but then retracted his action and sat in his chair, staring at his small figurines.

Juan went back to his room. He took his clothes off and began to get into his bed. Francisco was awake.

"Juan?" Francisco cautiously asked.

"What?" Juan responded with annoyance.

"I know what you did."

"What the hell are you talking about?" Juan asked.

"The cadets. I know now why they are so friendly with me."

"Don't know what you're talking about. Just go to sleep," Juan answered moodily.

"I just wanted to say thanks."

"Enough already. Just go to sleep and forget everything you know or think you know, all right?"

"Sure, Juan. Whatever you say."

Francisco listened to Juan and went back to sleep with a smile on his face. Francisco did not see that Juan had a little smirk on his face, but it was gone in an instant.

25

The Friend of My Friend Is My Enemy

As dawn approached the city of Churubusco, its light glowed through the flames caused by the fierce battle on the summit of Churubusco. The battle had been raging on for a while and was now coming to its climax. The final attack was to be led by Colonel Clifford. He had led the US forces into its final assault. The battle had begun in the early morning at the summit of Churubusco, where it seemed it would also end. The first assault was driven by William J. Worth and David E. Twiggs, with six thousand American soldiers. As the American army continued its successful campaign across Mexico, Pedro Maria Anaya still believed he could win the battle and would fight to the end. The Mexican Army managed to repel the particularly fierce attack by the Americans. Just as the main bridge looked likely to fall into American hands, there was still resistance from three small groups of Mexican and Irish militia known as the San Patricios. The San Patricios were deserters who had taken refuge in Mexico and joined its forces. A series of urgent messages had been dispatched by the Mexican Army for reinforcements but were intercepted by the Americans. The messages read, "Ran out of ammunition." As the American army attacked, wave after wave, many Mexican soldiers considered surrendering by raising the white flag over the Churubusco walls. They attempted it three times but were prevented from doing so by members of the San Patricios. The San Patricios feared for their fate, for they had once been part of the American army. Now branded as deserters, they knew what would happen if they were to fall into the hands of the American army. Even though the San Patricios were deserters, they felt a bond with the Mexican people.

The American army eventually won the battle. As the battle ended, John Clifford requested a status report from one of his captains.

"These are all the prisoners, sir. We separated the Mexican soldiers from the Irish scum. We have successfully captured seventy-two deserters, sir," the captain reported proudly.

Displeased with the sergeant's attitude, Clifford replied, "Very well, Captain. Continue to..." Clifford recognized a familiar face among the deserters. He saw an Irish soldier chained up with his head lowered. Clifford called out to him. "Jon Riley? Jon O'Riley?"

The prisoner looked up and replied, "John, is that you, you old war dog?"

"How did you...I mean, what have you done?" Clifford asked angrily, trying to grasp the severity of the situation.

"Long story, but you know me and my decisions. I don't make them lightly," Jon said as he stared into Clifford's eyes.

"I know that. You were always a wise lieutenant. That's why I ask." He noticed O'Riley's uniform had been altered. Clifford continued in a disapproving tone. "So you are fighting with the enemy now?"

"The enemy? Is that what they are now, John? Were they not our neighbors and friends at one point? And suddenly they become your enemy? Why? Why, John? Because a president with an agenda said so? I could not live with that. That's not why I joined the army, and you know it. If they are the enemy, then let me ask you one simple question. Who is watching out for your family at this very moment?"

"You know the answer to your question, and so do I. But even so, we took an oath. It is our duty when we put on this uniform," Clifford replied firmly.

"Yes, I remember. To serve God and country, duty and honor. But what happens when the army treats you worse than the enemy? My commander disciplined many of my men with corporal punishment for attending a Mexican mass. Where was the honor in that? Like I said, I joined to serve God and country, and my God does not recognize race. So neither do I. So, when I went to my commander, it was just the excuse he needed to accuse me and my men of treason. So we deserted. Many look down upon us because of our Irish descent. No, John. The army spat on my oath first. Therefore, I will stand by my decision." O'Riley finished with his chin held up high, waiting for the repercussions of his actions.

"You know the penalty for desertion. There's nothing I can do for you or your men," John responded sternly.

"Yes, I know, but I also know that Mexico gave me and my platoon a home. A home like the one we had when we lived in Ireland. I was just trying to protect it. You know what that means, John. We just wanted to protect something we were willing to fight to the death for." O'Riley looked away from John.

"I thought I did," a confused John Clifford answered as he looked down at O'Riley.

"This war is wrong. I think deep down inside you, you know this," O'Riley said to John as he looked back at him.

"I..." John could not respond to O'Riley's question. John then looked into O'Riley's eyes and saw a man who would die for his convictions.

General Scott, along with other commanders, was making his way to the prisoners to inspect them. He noticed Colonel Clifford staring at a prisoner.

"So, who do we have here?" General Scott asked.

"Sir, this is Jon O'Riley. He used to be a lieutenant in the US Army."

"Company K of the Fifth US Infantry Regiment, General," O'Riley interrupted with defiance.

"How far have we fallen, mixing it up with these Mexicans. Well, as a former enlisted man, you know what we do to deserters, don't you?" General Scott mocked, and then he addressed Clifford. "Continue assigning the punishment as soon as possible."

"But..."

"Why the hesitation, Colonel? This man is a deserter. You know what we do with deserters. We hang them, sir," Scott said loudly, trying to instill fear in the rest of the prisoners.

"But sir, I know this man. He would not have deserted if—"

"Do not waste your breath, Colonel. We all know how the general feels about deserters—or is it just Irish deserters?" O'Riley interrupted with mockery.

"I am done with you. Put a noose on him, Colonel," Scott ordered irritably.

"But sir, he is, or was, a lieutenant in the United States Army. To hang him without a trial would not be prudent," John replied.

The general thought about this for a moment, conferred with his entourage, and then said, "We are in a time of war, but you are right—for *now*. We will wait until we are close enough to Mexico City. He will get his trial, but we will then hang all his comrades whom we deemed guilty once we reach Chapultepec. Since they feel a bond with the Mexican people, it will be appropriate for them to die as we conquer Chapultepec. They will be hanged in the precise moment when the US flag replaces the Mexican one on top of the citadel, as a sign that you cannot escape death—especially from me," General Scott said in a pretentious tone.

"It would be an honor to die on Mexican soil, where I was truly free," O'Riley said with a sense of relief.

"Oh, no, Lieutenant, you shall not be hanged, for that is something you want. You will witness the hanging of your men. You will be issued a reminder of your treason. You will be branded with a *D* for your desertion. You will get your trial, but you will always be marked as a deserter."

General Scott added with indignation that his orders were to be followed.

26

With days passing by, many of the students at Chapultepec were getting a little restless. At noon, a mass of students began running toward the entrance of the castle like a herd of cattle. Cadets smiled as they witnessed the arrival of the Mexican Army. They had been apprehensive that reinforcements would not come in time. The cadets saluted the army as they filed into the castle. They sighed in relief as they witnessed this wonderful sight. As abruptly as it had begun, the cheers died down as the last soldiers piled into the castle. A total of five hundred men had marched through the castle's gates. Monterde greeted the two commanders, and they saluted each other.

"We are happy you were able to arrive in time; morale is currently low. Is the rest of the army far behind?" Monterde asked, waiting for a confirmation.

"No, General, this is all that is coming. General Santa Anna could not spare any more men at the moment," General Nicolas Bravo Rueda replied.

Monterde was stunned by Bravo's response but kept his composure. "Oh, I see. Well then, we welcome you and your soldiers. We will get your men some food and continue this conversation in my office."

"Thank you, General."

The men began their walk through the hallways. Some cadets continued to greet the incoming soldiers, while others observed them from a distance. From afar, Bara and Fernando were talking.

"How many do you count?" Fernando asked.

"I'm guessing about a little over five hundred men."

"So that makes 750 soldiers in total," Fernando replied apprehensively.

"And eighty cadets," Bara replied with discouragement.

"And eighty cadets," Fernando repeated desolately but caught himself. In an attempt to be optimistic, he said, "Well, I'm sure General Santa Anna will send more men."

"I suppose so," Bara replied.

"What's wrong?" Fernando asked, not wanting an answer.

"I…never mind. Let's go tend to their horses," Bara replied rapidly.

Juan Escutia joined Fernando and Bara on their way to tend the horses. Juan directed his attention toward Bara. Juan avoided any pleasantries with Fernando and seemed to be avoiding Fernando's line of sight.

"Bara, can I talk to you for a minute?"

"Certainly. What's wrong?" Bara asked.

"I need to talk to you. Alone," Juan said firmly.

"Hey, Juan, what's the matter?" Fernando interjected.

"Oh, hey, Fernando. Just wanted to ask Bara something important. I hope you don't mind."

"Oh, sure, no problem. I'm thirsty anyway. I'll be right back."

"Thanks, Fernando," Juan replied with a sense of relief. Fernando went to a well several feet away. He was now out of hearing distance, and Juan wanted to be sure he was far enough away so that he could to talk to Bara privately.

"So what's with all this secrecy?" Bara asked.

"Can you meet me at the stables tonight, around midnight?"

"Sure, but what's going on?"

"Just need to talk to someone. So if you can meet me, I would appreciate it." Juan was practically begging Bara.

"Sure, Juan. I'll meet you at midnight."

Fernando became restless and went back to Juan and Bara. Juan got anxious and left abruptly. As he left, he yelled out to Bara to confirm. "See you later, Bara."

Juan Escutia darted away without saying good-bye to Fernando.

"What was all that about?" Fernando asked Bara.

"I don't know. He just wants to talk to me later tonight."

"About what?"

"He didn't say. Well, let's get back to the stables."

Fernando's curiosity was getting the better of him, but he shrugged it off. The two cadets continued on their way to the stables.

27

General Monterde was in his office with his fellow commanders. They were all gathered around his desk, trying to figure a way to hinder the enemy's approach on the capital, but all their solutions were ineffective.

"The situation is impossible," General Monterde blurted out. "The Americans have more ammunition and men. There is still no response from General Santa Anna or from the capital. There seems to be no recourse but to have all the cadets leave the castle while there is still time. As the enemy is fast approaching, it is only a matter of time before they are here. We need to have the cadets assemble in the cathedral. I will address the men there. Now go," Monterde said in frustration.

28

All the cadets were gathered in the cathedral. They were uneasy as they waited for General Monterde. He entered the hall with a weary stride and began his address. "Gentlemen, I will spare you all the specifics of the American threat that is upon us. Suffice to say, we have agreed that the safety of our students comes first. So the first order of business is to ask all cadets in their first, second, or third years to prepare to leave the school immediately. I have received word that the enemy will soon be here. The Americans have defeated most of the army in Churubusco. Two days ago, they battled in *Molina de Rey* and destroyed our garrison and any chance to replenish our ammunition. We advise all of you to leave your posts immediately and return to your homes, to your loved ones. You will be much safer there than here. The soldiers will stay and defend the castle. The fourth-year cadets can choose to stay if they wish, considering all the training they have obtained. They have been equipped and trained to face the enemy and may do so if they wish. That is all for now."

As soon as Monterde finished, Bara stood up and looked at all the cadets around him. "Permission to speak, sir?" Bara asked bravely.

"Permission granted," Monterde said without hesitation, for he felt that a distraction from the upcoming events was most welcome.

"Sir, all the cadets have asked me and Vicente to speak on their behalf. We presumed this moment would come, and many of us have dreaded it. Every cadet knows the repercussions if we stay and fight. The majority of the cadets have decided they would gladly stay and fight together. If need be, we will die together."

Vicente then stood and continued the declaration. "Sir, many of us have decided to stand and fight. Time is not on our side, and it is now fleeting for many of us. That is why we want to make the most of it. I love my country. I will do anything for her. And if it means I have to fight to the death, then so be it. My heart keeps telling me one thing: to fight, and fight I will. *We* will. So we will fight for our country. We will fight for a free Mexico," Vicente said in a satisfied tone.

"Our hope is the same of those before us—to have our country be free from tyranny. We can't just let that hope slip away. The Americans are not invading just a castle. They are not invading an academy. They are invading our home. Many of us believe Santa Anna will still come to our aid. So we will stay," Bara said.

As the general looked at his cadets, he knew deep down he could not persuade them to leave, even if he gave them the order to do so.

"Do you all feel this way?" Monterde said with encouragement.

All the cadets stood and said in unison, "YES, SIR!"

"Then we fight tomorrow. For country, for pride, for Mexico!" Monterde responded.

"Viva MEXICO!" they all said in unison.

29

Later that night, Juan Escutia was at the stables waiting for his friend Bara to arrive. Walking back and forth, Juan was rehearsing what he wanted to say. He even practiced to the horse standing before him. Juan brushed the horse and patted its neck. This made Juan smile a bit. Then Bara entered and greeted him. Juan bent down and picked up a bottle of tequila to offer Bara a drink.

"Thanks for meeting me here," Juan said appreciatively.

"Why all the secrecy?" Bara asked.

"We will get to that. Take a drink." Juan tried to express a sense of open-mindedness to Bara.

"All right, just one drink." Bara took a swig.

"What's the hurry? I brought some food as well."

"Listen, if you are anxious about tomorrow…"

"It's not that," Juan said eagerly.

"Well, then what? We now have strict orders. We need our energy for tomorrow."

"I know. But I don't think *we* are the priority right now, if you know what I mean."

Bara agreed and took another swig from the bottle of tequila.

"Where in hell did you get this?" Bara gasped.

"I have a secret stash. It's all I could get. Now, did it do the trick?"

"Oh, yeah," Bara replied, coughing in a high pitch.

"Hey, Bara," Juan said with more confidence.

"Yeah?" Bara replied, feeling the effects of the alcohol.

"Remember when you told me about your father?"

"Yes," Bara replied, not paying attention.

"And then you asked about mine, but I would always change the topic?"

"Yeah, so?" Bara said as he took his third drink.

"Well, if we are going to die tomorrow, I want you to know something. It's hard for me to say, but I will go ahead and tell you. Agustin mentioned the Diablos, remember?"

"That's the group of bandits in the Sierra Madre that killed Fernando's parents," Bara replied.

"My father is in the gang. He goes through the country-side terrorizing innocent people," Juan said, and waited for a reaction.

"Juan, why are you telling me this?" Bara replied in disbelief.

"Because my father is their leader. It was he who killed Fernando's parents. When Fernando described how his parents died, I knew it was him. I just can't deal with the fact that, because of my father, Fernando's parents are dead. My father made him an orphan," Juan said in anguish. He stood up with both of his fists clinched.

Bara tried to console Juan. "Even if that's all true, you didn't kill them. He did." Bara walked over to Juan and put his hand on his shoulder.

"I know that deep inside, but it does not change how I feel. What I didn't know was that he was also an officer in the military."

Bara was shocked.

Juan continued. "He fought alongside Monterde during the war. Monterde told me he was an excellent soldier, perhaps too good a soldier. After the war, his love for battle drove my father insane. He just continued to kill people. If only he would have died in those famous battles, he would have died a hero. Now he's known as a murdering bandit. And what keeps me awake every night, what scares me the most, is that I might be like him." Juan looked down at his palms and continued. "Considering the same blood that flows through his veins flows through mine."

Bara again tried to console Juan. "But you are not your father."

"It won't change how the world will see me because of who my father is. All I want is to be half the man General Monterde is. How could I ever break free from my father's shadow? His sins? His legacy will continue to follow me wherever I go," Juan said in a distressed tone. He slumped over with his face buried in his hands.

"You said it, Juan. His sins. Juan, do you remember what the general told us? A man can change his destiny," Bara said, trying to sympathize with Juan.

Juan faced Bara and pointed to his chest. "My destiny has already been written. There's no place for me here now. All I ever wanted was to believe in something. I promised God a long time ago, that if he could help me break free from his cycle of terror, Mexico would become my family. I would be a true son of Mexico if only I could grab hold of that hope the general talked about." Juan was exasperated as he tried to hold his tears in.

Bara looked at him with compassion and squeezed his shoulder. "For what it's worth, I'm proud of you. It took guts for you to tell me everything," Bara said.

"Yeah, but what about Fernando? He has a right to know that it was my father who killed his parents. I want to tell him, but I just feel so hollow inside. I feel like everyone has abandoned me, including God."

"No, I think God is with us now more than ever," Bara said confidently.

"How do you figure?" Juan asked.

"No matter what happens, I am at peace. I will be all right in the end," Bara said confidently, as if he were talking to himself.

"I wish I could have what you have," Juan said. He was jealous of Bara's position.

"You just have to ask for it. And, about telling Fernando, I really don't know. I guess there will be a right time for you to tell him. But for now, just try to get some rest. Tomorrow I have to prepare the forest entrance and dig trenches. Just remember what I said," Bara ordered, trying to ease Juan's anguish.

"Thanks, Bara. I really mean it," Juan said candidly. Bara's words did touch Juan. He saluted Bara. Bara saluted back with a smile.

The boys went back to their dorm rooms. But in the shadows of the stable, a distinctive figure stepped out, and the moonlight brightened up the figure. It was Fernando, and he had heard everything. He stared at the ground and clenched his fists.

30

Provoked

As the American army approached in the early morning, the thunder of their horses reached the castle. Many students were already up and about, but were taken aback by the massive army they saw approaching. Off to the east side of the castle, Bara was diligently completing his assignment of digging an enormous trench from the side of the castle closest to the forest. When he heard the approaching army, he stopped to see the Americans but then resumed his task. The cadets inside the castle had a better view, and with them was General Monterde. He saw the army of thirteen thousand men strong.

"So it begins," Monterde said to himself.

It took the entire day for the American army to arrive, start camping out, and arrange their tents and cannons. One of the many tents housed General Scott, and he was there assessing his battle plans. General Scott was not alone. He was accompanied by his council of officers and engineers as they continued to plot their attack on the castle.

"We cannot go around the castle due to the steep hills that it sits on. So we must attack from the south side," General Scott advised.

"I concur with your assessment, sir," Robert Lee replied.

"Once we take over the castle, we can set in motion our march through the gates of Mexico City," Scott said with a premature smile.

"General, can we attack from the southwest entrance of the forest and then proceed to north side entrance?" Colonel Clifford asked.

"Yes, but not by way of our heavy artillery. Due to the dense forest, we cannot get all our cannons through. Nor can we get a clean shot to the main target, the castle. No, at nightfall, we will establish the heavy batteries to lead the infantry within easy range of the castle. I will not waste time, nor offer them a choice to surrender. Begin bombardment immediately after sunrise."

"When do you want the infantry to advance, sir?" Clifford asked, to ensure all the men were on the same page.

"The cannons alone will do. With so many missiles crippling them from the north side, I doubt there will be any Mexican soldiers left for resistance. But have the men stand by, ready for any of the Mexican soldiers trying to escape," Scott said decisively.

31

When night fell, it crept over the forest with an eerie darkness. American forces were beginning to move their cannons into position. While they were doing this, many of the cadets in the castle were planning their own strategy. General Monterde's council was discussing its own battle plans. Other cadets were in their rooms resting for the next day's engagement. They would all need their rest. A few cadets found solace inside the chapel. Many were sitting and praying—particularly Francisco de Oca, who sat and prayed in a whisper. "God, grant me the strength and courage for what I am about to face. Please instill peace into every one of our cadets. I thank thee, O Lord."

Juan entered his dorm room to get ready for guard duty that night. As he put his uniform on, he noticed Francisco's father's knife on his bunk. A note was attached to it. Juan picked up the knife and read the note:

> *Juan, since we have different duty times, we most*
> *likely won't see each other tomorrow. I just want you*

to know that I tried to be a great soldier like you, but I know I was lacking in that. I must admit there were times when I thought you were hard on me, to make me a better soldier. Even though I didn't become more like you, in appreciation I thought you might want my father's knife. He would have wanted a real soldier to have it. Besides, I still have his cross, and that's all I really need. I had hoped that we could be friends. It was great being your roommate. Francisco.

Juan hung his head and sat down on his bunk. He stared at the floor. He then stood up and left the room with Francisco's knife.

32

The next day, the sun's rays extended over the land and General Scott's tent. As he emerged, he looked anxiously over his army. General Scott did not want to waste any time. He walked away from his tent well dressed and ordered his men to position themselves for the commencement of the bombardment. The army proceeded to get into position.

General Scott began to address his men. "Today is a wonderful day for victory. I will be brief, men. I want that castle. You have this morning to get it. And when you get it, I will enjoy the rest of my day basking victoriously in the center of the castle. We will be victorious. Many great stories will be told of what we do today. Be proud, men. For when we return to the States, they will see us as heroes. Your children will look up to you as great men who shaped our great nation. Colonel, prepare for battle."

"You heard the general. Prepare to fire the cannons," Colonel Clifford responded.

The soldiers began the bombardment of the castle, but they were missing their target. Many of the cannons were hitting the trees and not doing any real damage at all. General Scott grew impatient. His eyes pierced through every soldier.

"Rectify the aim, Colonel Mackenzie. And you, Lieutenant, get those men into position, for they are thirty degrees off their mark. Colonel Clifford, I expect much better productivity from you."

"Yes, sir. You heard the general."

The aim was fixed, and the castle's walls were now taking many hits. Yet the walls were very much fortified. One wall was now on fire, but it was contained; there was no real damage. Parts of the castle's roof were damaged, but it held its integrity. The American army continued to bombard the castle but could not advance. When the bombing stopped, the infantry tried to advance up the steep cliffs. The Mexican soldiers and cadets in the castle stood their ground, forcing the American soldiers to rethink this strategy. Winfield Scott continued to be frustrated by the castle's defenses.

In the castle, the cadets were scrambling to defend their stations. Some were protecting the front gates, while others were in ditches they had dug in the forest. In a ditch facing the east side of the castle were Francisco and Agustin.

"What if Santa Anna does not come with reinforcements? Will we have to fight to the death?" Francisco asked.

"Do not focus on that. We have to concentrate on fighting. We have come this far, and nothing can stop this."

"I just wish I could have seen my mother to tell her one last thing," Francisco said desperately, as he held his cross in one hand.

"Many of us would have liked to talk to our loved ones one last time. What would you tell her?" Agustin said, trying to help Francisco keep his mind off the situation.

"That I hope she understands why I stayed, and..." Francisco got all choked up and couldn't continue.

"And?" Agustin asked, trying to get Francisco to forget the imminent attack.

"Just hoping I made her proud," he replied doubtfully. Francisco tried to compose himself.

"I have no doubt that is exactly how she feels," Agustin said.

"I shouldn't be scared, but I am," Francisco said as he looked at Agustin.

"Well, I can't help you there because I'm scared as well. But I do remember what the general told me when I lost my parents. Death is a natural thing, and it comes to us all. It's how we face it that matters. So if death comes to us now, we will make our stand and fight to the end."

"Then I am with you," Francisco said with a sense of purpose as Agustin's words revitalized him.

"Prepare yourself, then, for here they come!" Agustin yelled as he prepared to take aim at the enemy now approaching.

Agustin, Francisco, and the rest of the cadets began firing at the approaching soldiers. Back at the castle, other cadets saw the American army trying to infiltrate the walls, but the cadets succeeded in stopping them. The cadets exhibited courage that was to be respected. As they patiently aimed their weapons, they picked off their enemy one by one. While the bombs continued to barrage over the castle, the cadets were still holding their positions. The American soldiers continued trying to breach the castle walls but failed time and time again. Sunset was fast approaching, and the American army had to fall back. The cadets began cheering when they saw the last of the American soldiers retreat back to their base. General Monterde had a smile on his face as he witnessed his enemy's retreat.

33

Reevaluation

General Scott was furious with the results of his first wave of attacks. He had not expected the Mexican defenses to hold the way they had against his army. The night came far too early to continue the assault.

The cadets had been able to stop the Americans for now. The entrances and sides of the castle had not been breached. The American force could not advance.

Bara was relieved from his station at the forest entrance. He went into the castle and to General Monterde's office to continue to plan his defense. As he walked through the castle, he saw many cadets tending to other cadets and soldiers who had been injured in the American assault. Bara witnessed cadets not being able to rest or sleep because the sound of the cannons was still echoing in their ears. The cooks were handing out a few rations. Many of the cadets knew it might be their last meal. Once Bara got to Monterde's office, he was surrounded by several men at the table. General Monterde reported the current status to his men.

"We were able to stop them here, here, and here. The steep climb from the cliffs discouraged the Americans, but I don't think that will be the case tomorrow. The walls are weakened. I feel they will continue to do the same tomorrow but with much more effectiveness. I suspect they will attack without preconception. If they proceed and are able to come over the walls, they will have a level fighting field. We cannot allow that to happen. We need to have strongholds planted here and here. They will also try to come through the main gate and the southwest side of the forest. Beware of the cannons, since they will have made adjustments to their aim. But as soon as they stop and advance with their infantry, we will stop them here and here. Our food supplies, as well as our ammunition, are almost gone. Be wise with your shots. I have reports that many cadets have lost their spirit with the absence of reinforcements. Are there any suggestions to help the cadets with their morale?"

"Well, we could say that the Americans want to surrender, but we refused their offer since none of us speak English," Bara said, trying to lighten the mood.

"We could also say General Santa Anna will not be joining us for breakfast tomorrow, so more food for us?" Agustin interrupted with a smile.

"I need real solutions, not jokes. My men—your men—are dying out there. If I am to die out there, I want…we might all die tomo…" General Monterde answered with frustration. The cadets and soldiers all stood still. Even though humor was being used, Monterde was able to see fear in the eyes of his fellow men. He began to realize the cadets knew one thing for sure: they would, most likely, all die tomorrow. The cadets needed a way to relieve the stress, and, considering the current situation, why not with laughter?

"Well, cadets, if we die tomorrow, then we die laughing in death's face," Monterde responded.

"Sir, shall death be our last lesson?" Bara asked Monterde in a tone not meant to be humorous. It was asked to confirm what was most likely going to occur the next day.

"I have taught you all many things, but death was not in the curriculum. I have been in many difficult situations, but never with the lives of children in my hands. You asked about death. Many see death as an ending or a beginning. But if you face yours tomorrow, you will decide how it will end. For death comes to us all. It is how we face death that reflects on how we lived."

As soon as the commander said this, peace fell on the faces of the cadets.

"I need to address everyone. Gather all the men and cadets at the cathedral."

It did not take long for the men to gather. Though many were weary, they all stood at attention, waiting for Monterde to address them.

He began. "I know many of you are tired and discouraged due to the lack of support from the capital and General Santa Anna. Many of you are hungry. Many of you are afraid. There is no shame in that. I have had many brave men fight by my side who felt the same way you do. Now I have young cadets who have the same strength as those soldiers. So if I am to die tomorrow, I will die proudly by your side. You are sons of Mexico, and we will fight like men with valor. We will let our enemies know that they cannot destroy our hopes and dreams of a united Mexico." As Monterde said this, there was no applause, no cheering, but a spirit of rejuvenation and hope fell on everyone. Monterde resumed. "Let us pray."

All the cadets bowed their heads and recited the Lord's Prayer in unison. "Our Father, who art in heaven, hallowed be thy name..."

34

The early morning of September 13, 1847 came too soon for both parties. The battle fought the day before had not gone as planned for General Scott. He had clearly misjudged the Mexican defense. Scott decided to change his offensive action. He ordered the proper adjustments to the cannons during the night. This time, he would begin with a cannon assault as well as a full infantry assault. It would be an unexpectedly bold move. An exasperated Scott gave the order to his men in his command center.

"This time, we will fire as soon as the sun rises. Then we will make an assault straight up the cliffs. The cannons will give them cover while they advance."

"I understand, sir, but won't the fragments of the cannons fall upon our soldiers?" Colonel Clifford asked.

"I want that castle, Colonel. I will do whatever I deem necessary to win this war," General Scott said firmly.

"Colonel Mackenzie will storm the castle with his party where the three assault columns lay," George Cadwalader said.

"Excellent, sir," General Scott said. "Have Trousdale and Johnston move up the flanks."

"Very well, General," Cadwalader replied.

"That is all. Get your troops ready. Victory shall be ours today. All are dismissed, except for Colonel Clifford."

The other colonels and lieutenants left. Clifford began to address General Scott first. "I'm sorry if I spoke out of turn, sir, but there is a chance we could end up with a high mortality rate," Lieutenant Clifford said apologetically.

"I am well aware of what I am doing. Do not ever dispute my orders in front of others. Is that clear, Colonel?" Scott said.

"Yes, sir," Clifford said courteously.

"Very well. Dismissed."

Colonel Clifford left General Scott and made his men assemble to relay the orders he had just received.

"All right, gentlemen. I have orders that the infantry will attack straight up the cliffs at first light. We will aid you with the cannons."

When the colonel finished addressing his men, they just stood there. Muttering began among them. One by one, they began to voice their disagreement of the order. Colonel Clifford took charge when he saw the men were beginning to look at one another with hesitation.

"Now listen well, men, for I will say this only once. You will take this castle. You will engage the enemy, and you will be victorious. The mortars will go over your heads. We made the appropriate corrections last night. Do not fear, men. Have faith in God and our commander. Are you with me?" Clifford said with authority. Only some men cheered in agreement. Clifford added, "I believe that we have the same tenacity of our forefathers. We will breach the castle. We will continue to be victorious."

This time, all his men agreed.

The cannons began firing at sunrise. The effects of the blasts began to weaken the castle walls. Many of the soldiers and cadets in the castle began to scatter, room to room, corridor to corridor. Many cadets were immobile, since they knew that if they moved in the wrong direction, it could mean their lives. The cannons seemed more intense than the previous day. With no sign of Santa Anna, the cadets began to realize there would be only one outcome for them today. Some cadets peered through the holes the cannonballs made in the walls and saw something very unusual. The American army was starting to climb upward toward the castle while their cannons continued to fire.

Colonel Clifford continued to give orders. "Get those cannons into place."

General Scott approached Clifford. "Now, Colonel, I said a full infantry assault."

"General, I—" Clifford said doubtfully.

"This is your final warning, Colonel. Now, obey my command," General Scott said, flustered.

"Yes, sir. Begin the full advance now. Go, go."

All the troops were now advancing toward the cliffs while the cannons were shooting. As predicted by Colonel Clifford, the effects of the cannons were connecting with some of the soldiers. Desperately, Clifford ordered his captains to have their men aim with accuracy.

"Aim higher to the point over their heads. You, Captain, order your men to aim higher."

"Sir, we are doing the best we can," the captain responded.

"Do better, Captain. Those are your comrades out there," Clifford responded with a sense of urgency.

"Yes, Colonel," the captain said in desperation. The casualties were minimal with the adjustments, but there were still some scattered men being injured by the debris caused by the cannons. The infantry was now advancing to the northeast, and sharpshooters were advancing to the north and east entrances of the castle. The American forces were entering more into the castle's territory. General Scott's plan was working. The American army was able to advance into the castle more easily.

The cadets were having trouble of their own, especially from their own cannons. Bara rode into the castle to give a status report. He got off his horse and headed toward Monterde.

"What is going on with those cannons, Captain?" Monterde asked Captain Juarez.

"Sir, the cannons are now misfiring."

A cadet came running to General Monterde, interrupting.

"Sir, the land mines are failing to explode. We might have confused the type of fuses we needed last night, sir. They must have been the ones that were meant to be destroyed due to corrosion," the cadet reported.

Then another cadet ran to the three men in the courtyard. "The enemy is now advancing, sir," the cadet said, catching his breath.

"Have the men continue to hold their positions until the final moment when the enemy comes over the walls. Then fall back to the center of the school. That is where we will make our last stand. I want every cadet to fall back," Monterde said.

"Sir, the forest entry is beginning to be breached. The men are too far away to retreat. With the enemy fast approaching, I say they don't have much time. I doubt that the cadets can get back to the center of the castle as well," a captain reported to Monterde and Bara.

Bara looked at Monterde and with a sense of urgency said, "Sir, that entrance was my responsibility. I will go and stand by my men. I will not leave my unit. I will make my stand there until the end, and if I can free some of the cadets to allow them to fall back, I will."

"Very well, son. Godspeed," Monterde answered Bara.

Bara ran to his horse nearby and galloped to Monterde. "Thank you, General, for everything." Bara added, "It has been a great learning experience. I am glad to have met you and served under your command."

"Juan De La Barrera, you have far surpassed your father's shadow," General Monterde said as Juan was about to ride away. With a stern and upright posture, General Monterde saluted young Bara.

Bara paused for a second and saluted back. His face clenched, he yelled to his horse, "Yea!"

Bara galloped out of the castle, avoiding several American soldiers trying to either shoot him or pull him off. Bara made his way to the forest. He rode with great speed.

As soon as Bara was out of sight, a young cadet yelled to General Monterde, "Sir, they are now flanking us from the south entrance. Their numbers are superior to ours."

Vicente emerged from one of the halls that was filled with smoke. He ran to Monterde. "Sir, they are breaching our walls and are climbing over."

"Everyone back to the center of the courtyard and find cover," Monterde ordered.

The cadets moved toward the center of the castle, in full retreat. The Americans were now within the castle walls and shooting without bias. As American soldiers were either running in the castle or engaging cadets in the courtyard, a few Mexican soldiers could not retreat and were trapped on the edges of the walls. They would now fight till the end.

Juan Escutia was trapped as a barrage of bullets hailed upon him. Fernando saw this and took full advantage of Juan's situation. Fernando took aim at Juan. He thought justice would finally be served. The blood that Juan's father had spilled would be replaced by his son's. If Fernando were to shoot, would he finally find peace? Could he come to terms with such an outcome? Fernando breathed calmly and realized that Juan was pinned down by an American sharpshooter. Fernando took aim, and Juan was now also in the American's sight.

Fernando yelled in a great anger that Juan could hear clearly, "Juan Escutia, son of the leader of Los Diablos!"

Juan heard Fernando and was shocked as he realized that Fernando was pointing his rifle straight at him.

"Duck!" Fernando yelled out again.

Juan reacted just as Fernando aimed and shot the sharpshooter, who had Juan in his crosshairs. The bullet went right through the head of the sharpshooter. Fernando ran to Juan. Juan was still reacting to his almost-imminent demise. He saw Fernando approaching him and said, "Well, that was close." Juan waited for a reaction from Fernando. Fernando began to smile, and Juan realized Fernando was not going to react gravely.

Juan resumed talking. "Listen, before I get into another situation like that, I need to tell you something."

"I know everything," Fernando told Juan and added, "There's nothing left to say."

"How long have you known?" Juan asked.

"Long enough. All I know is that you are a good soldier and a good friend. That is all I ever need to know," Fernando replied. He had come to terms with his anger toward Juan's father.

"I'm so sorry. I wanted to tell you since I found out," Juan said remorsefully.

"Don't worry about it. It could have been worse. Your father could have been Bara's father."

The two boys smiled, and Juan began to chuckle. As Fernando smiled, he suddenly jerked toward Juan. He slowly stopped smiling. Fernando looked up at Juan and muttered, "Juan I...I've been shot."

As he said this, Fernando looked down at his chest and saw blood clotting through his clothes. He fell toward Juan. Juan took hold of Fernando.

"Funny thing is, I don't feel anything," Fernando muttered.

Juan continued to hold Fernando so he wouldn't fall straight to the ground. Juan pulled his hand out from behind Fernando's back and saw blood all over his hand. He fell backward with Fernando's weight and noticed that a bullet had just missed him. Juan saw the direction of the shot. He took Fernando's rifle and took aim at where he believed the shot had come from. Juan saw that the sniper was about to shoot right at him. He shot first, killing the sniper. He then focused back on Fernando.

"Fernando, stay with me. I'm going to get you out of here," Juan said nervously as he tried to stop the bleeding.

"Don't bother, Juan. I'm dying. Just as well, you know. I now realize that we each have our own destiny to follow. We shouldn't ignore what is meant for us," Fernando said as he began to weaken.

"Fernando, stay with me," Juan demanded as blood now completely covered his hands. The shot was a mortal wound.

"Just keep that promise you made to God. You know, the one you told Juan about in the stables," Fernando said weakly.

"Don't talk. I'm going to get you out of here," Juan said desperately as he saw blood continuing to flow out of Fernando's back.

"Just ask God for the peace you so much desire, and let go of the hate you have for your father. Remember, you truly are a son of Mexico. I just wish I could have..." Fernando died in Juan's arms. Juan laid his friend gently on the ground.

Hunched over Fernando's body, he noticed the enemy had breached the castle. Juan looked up and saw the Americans had also breached the top of the castle. They were attempting to lower the Mexican flag from the citadel.

35

As Bara rode furiously across the forest, he had the ditch he had made with his comrades in sight. Bara saw the American forces were now advancing closely with their small cannons. They were bombing the trenches where Bara's post was. Bara himself was avoiding the oncoming projectiles, zigzagging through the forest. The Americans saw him from afar. One projectile came so close to Bara that his horse threw him off, and he fell to the ground. His horse was dead. Bara ran to the trench and jumped in with his fellow cadets. He noticed many were wounded.

"How many cadets are dead?" Bara asked.

"About seven, sir!" Agustin responded sadly.

"And injured?"

"Ten."

"Continue firing. While we are firing, I want you to fall back to the castle with the wounded," Bara said firmly and without hesitation, hoping none would see his desperation.

"But sir, we are almost out of gunpowder," a cadet responded.

As soon as he said this, Agustin added, "Bara, we just ran out of ammo for the cannons."

"Then listen carefully. The enemy will be advancing toward us now. If you are able to walk and are not injured, I want you to help the wounded cadets and fall back to the castle now," Bara ordered with a pleading tone.

Many cadets grabbed what they could and prepared to leave, but there were those who stood still, frozen with fear.

"But sir, won't the enemy begin shooting at us as soon as we leave the trench?" a frightened cadet asked.

"We will cover you as much as we can. Now go. I gave you all an order," Bara said harshly.

"What about you, Bara?" Agustin asked with apprehension.

"I will stay here with any volunteers and defend this last line of defense as long as we can. Now go."

"Let's just surrender," a cadet yelled in desperation.

"Yes, yes, let's give up, and maybe they won't kill us," another cadet agreed.

"Is that what you want? All of you?" Bara responded furiously.

Bara looked at the young men and saw fear in their eyes. He was about to yell at them but suddenly realized many were staring at something right above his head, toward the castle. Bara turned around to see what they were all gazing at. They all stood in silence and watched their flag being lowered from the citadel.

The silence was broken by a cadet uttering the obvious. "Sir, the Americans are lowering our flag."

They continued to stare at the rooftop of the castle and saw their flag receding to its base.

36

Back at the castle, the American army was engaging in hand-to-hand combat with the rest of the Mexican cadets and soldiers. The Americans had now scaled the walls with wave after wave of men. The overwhelming American force was taking full advantage of what was left of the remaining Mexican soldiers. The American soldiers, with their superior numbers, began bayoneting the cadets and throwing the lifeless bodies over the castle's cliffs. The cadets who had fallen back to the center of the courtyard saw their comrades fall into the hands of the enemy. As the cadets and soldiers continued to die, the sight frightened the cadets even more. Many soldiers in the American army were now in position to take prisoners.

General Monterde was at the center of the castle behind the main gate, maintaining his ground. It was just a matter of time before the American troops collided with him and his men.

"Men, prepare for engagement," Monterde yelled. He wanted to say something to motivate his cadets but was at a loss for words. He saw fear beginning to set in the cadet's hearts. The realization of death was too much for them. Some cadets began to weep.

Monterde shouted out orders. "Form two lines of defense, here and here. You there, get behind that post. And you, Cadet, reload your weapon."

As the general gave the orders to his men, he knew many would not continue the fight. They were drained from no sleep and hunger, and now fear. The general prayed for a miracle.

"Sir, the Americans are on top of the citadel," a cadet yelled as he pointed to the top of the citadel. They all looked up and saw the commotion but could not quite see what was happening.

"Sir, where is our flag?" a cadet asked Monterde.

"Is this the end, General? What do we do now?" another cadet bellowed out.

The general just looked up with loathing at the absence of his flag. "Is this how it ends? Did I sacrifice the lives of these children for a dream so out of reach?" Monterde thought. Then doubt started to creep into his mind.

37

General Scott was getting ready to make a grand entrance into the castle. As the general prepared himself, Colonel Clifford entered his tent. Colonel Clifford stood in front of the general silently, holding back his anger. The general saw Clifford struggling to say a word and wondered what was on his mind.

"What is it, Colonel? I did not call for you. Can't you see I am getting ready for my victory? It won't be long since the castle is completely breached and all mine. Do you have something to report?"

"I thought the general would like to know his current status."

"Very well. What do you have for me?"

"Two hundred and seventy-five dead and one hundred and thirty-two wounded, sir!"

"Very well, Colonel. Release a detail to have the Mexican casualties removed from my entrance. I do not want their smell to reach me as I enter the castle."

"These reports are for our side, sir. The cannons did most of the damage."

Scott turned around, and his eyes pierced into Clifford.

Not backing down, Clifford resumed his report. "I just thought the general would like to know the repercussions of his actions," Clifford responded mockingly.

"Clifford, too many times I have warned you," Scott replied roughly.

"And yes, we have breached the castle. We infiltrated the castle, and the Mexican flag on top of the citadel will be lowered anytime now," Clifford said grudgingly, for he knew what was to happen next.

"Then what are you waiting for? Prepare the deserters for their punishment," Scott responded without batting an eye.

"Sir, I beg you to reconsider. We can still wait until we go back home. These are good men," Clifford answered, with hope that there might be a way to save the deserters. At least until they could get a fair hearing.

"We must obey the rules of war. You of all people know this, Colonel."

General Scott called out for a major. As he came into the tent, the general addressed the major. "Major, prepare the hanging of those traitors. Once you see the Mexican flag completely descended, you have my orders to implement their sentence."

"Yes, General, right away," the major replied as he left the tent.

"General, I have children, and I have tried to teach them right from wrong. And I believe this to be wrong. I made a promise to them that I would be a just man. But I feel this was not a just war, and I fear God will not be with me at the end of this life," Clifford said with restlessness.

"Well, then. Because of your convictions, I will save you from such a dilemma. As of now, you are relieved of your duties."

Clifford was surprised at first but was pleased. "Thank you, sir," he responded with a sigh of gratitude.

"Like it or not, we are very much alike. We are both men of God, who put God and country first."

"Hardly, sir, for I fear God. The general fears nothing nor feels nothing. I hope to God I am nothing like the general," Clifford said sharply.

"Funny how you mentioned God. For it is he who sent us here, to this particular military school," Scott responded righteously.

"You are wrong sir; it was not God but a blind president who sent us here. And what do you mean a military school? We thought the castle was a military headquarters," a baffled Clifford responded.

"That is what we first thought. We then received information it was just a school that housed Mexican students. I did not want any of my soldiers having any doubts in attacking the castle knowing that children were in it," Scott said smugly.

"With all due respect, sir, you repulse me," Clifford replied angrily.

General Scott then pierced Clifford's eyes and responded, "Like it or not, God is with us in this war. We are doing his will, and our actions are blessed by God himself."

"Unlike the general, I am mortified by what I have done. I, for one, will not hide behind God to justify my actions,"

Clifford said. And for a split second, he saw a glimpse of doubt in General Scott's eyes.

Scott was speechless. He had every intention of calling a guard to have Clifford taken away. But General Scott could only reply by stating, "You are dismissed, Colonel."

38

Undying Hope

Juan Escutia arrived at the top of the citadel. He saw two American soldiers lowering his country's flag. As they did, they were talking to each other. Juan heard them clearly. "Tell me again why we broke from our unit?" one soldier asked.

"If we capture the flag, we'll be the famous ones," the other American soldier replied excitedly.

"Oh, well, I don't mind a bit of glory. Bring it down faster," the soldier said now, happily.

As the two American soldiers continued to lower the flag, they heard an infuriated Juan yelling at them, "*Hijos de puta.*"

One of the American soldiers was taken by surprise and began looking for his weapon. The other soldier knew where his rifle was and was about to shoot at Juan, but Juan knelt down and shot the soldier first. The dead soldier keeled over. Fernando's rifle was very accurate, and Juan had good aim.

Juan pulled out his sword for the other soldier. The soldier was now ready with his rifle and took aim at Juan. It did not frighten Juan, and he leaped forward with rage. The American soldier pulled the trigger, but his rifle misfired. Realizing his predicament, he reacted to Juan's attack and blocked his charge.

The soldier took the offensive and lunged forward at Juan with his bayonet. The two men fought with ferocity. The soldier swung his bayonet and missed Juan. Juan swung his sword and scraped the soldier's arm. This attack angered the American so much that he lunged toward Juan and pushed him onto his back. As Juan fell backward, the American lunged his bayonet for a kill strike toward Juan.

Juan remembered he had Francisco's knife in his back pocket. He retrieved the knife and threw it with all his might right into the soldier's stomach. The soldier stopped and looked down at the handle of the knife sticking out of his stomach. He looked up, and the last thing he saw was Juan swooshing his sword across his neck. The soldier's head was completely cut off. The body fell limp onto the ground.

Juan fell back to the ground to catch his breath. He saw the Mexican flag lying on the ground and went toward it. As he picked it up, he saw that it was stained with his and the dead soldier's blood. Then it dawned on him what his flag represented. Juan pulled the flag with both hands up to his face, and he began to cry. As soon as he started, he stopped, smiled, and looked up to the heavens. With the flag in his hands, Juan stretched his arms toward the sky. Sunlight poured on his face. He fell to his knees and retracted his arms. He said to himself, "Thank you. I am at peace now. I know my destiny."

Juan heard several men approaching up the stairs, most likely the rest of the dead soldier's unit. Juan knew he was outnumbered and would die once the soldiers got there. His first instinct was to fight. When he looked at Fernando's rifle, he realized he was out of bullets. He then focused on the flag in his hands. He got up and stood right at the edge of the castle. With a sense of tranquility sweeping over his body, a smile appeared on his face. He draped the flag over his body. Despite all the smoke, he saw that the fire had produced a beautiful glimmer of light. He took one last look at the forest. He noticed many of his fellow cadets were watching him from a distance. The Americans reached the entrance to the roof-top as Juan turned to face them. The soldiers saw their fellow soldiers lying dead on the ground. Seeing Juan's feats, they all took aim at him. Slowly, the American soldiers prepared to fire.

Juan smiled. The American soldiers held their fire in astonishment as they saw Juan rewrap the flag over himself and leap off the castle's edge. He smiled one last time and closed his eyes as he fell to his death, landing on the jagged rocks below. The Americans were taken aback by such an act.

39

As the Americans continued to engage the remaining Mexican cadets, they began to realize their enemy was nothing more than children. They expected to see the same adult soldiers they had fought in Veracruz and Monterrey. A few soldiers admired such fierce fighting from the Mexican Army in past battles. Now, they were fighting children and were hesitating. The moment was fleeting, and the American soldiers continued to battle and advance into the castle.

As General Monterde and his soldiers witnessed Juan Escutia's death, a jolt went through General Monterde, and he thought, "I guess you found your hope, son. Thank you for giving mine back."

Many of the tired cadets were now in shock after witnessing Juan's leap.

"They don't deserve to touch our flag," a cadet said in anger as tears streamed down his face.

"Juan had the right idea. Let us all fight to the end," another cadet yelled.

"I will die before I see an American flag raised in my country," Cadet Miramon yelled out.

"Then prepare for your destiny, men," Monterde said, and his eyes welled up as he yelled out the order.

The American force had breached the barriers where Monterde was making his stand.

"Find whatever you can and use it. Let them know we will not go quietly," General Monterde ordered as his emotions got the better of him. Monterde began shooting. Many of the cadets had run out of bullets. Some of them were picking up rocks and sticks, anything that could be used as a weapon. Every cadet was now fighting hand-to-hand combat, to the death. The general noticed his men had no fear and was proud of them. Monterde focused back on his enemy and fought with fierceness. Just as Monterde was about to take another American soldier's life, he was hit from behind with the butt of an American rifle. Monterde fell to the ground and was barely conscious as blood began to flow from his head. Monterde continued to see his young cadets fighting as he lay on the ground.

"My, what a glorious sight. Fight on, my tin soldiers," Monterde muttered to himself. He could not maintain consciousness and closed his eyes as a single tear fell across his face.

Vicente fired his weapon until he ran out of bullets. He was shot in the arm and was ordered to stop by the Americans. But he ignored the order and continued to fight. Vicente was shot once again in the shoulder and stabbed in the stomach by an American soldier with a bayonet. He put his hand over his wound and tried to stand but staggered. He wanted to continue to fight. Vicente was shot one last time and fell on his stomach. He clutched the ground and tried to push himself up but was only able to get onto his knees.

"*Viva la independencia!*" Vicente cried out. When he said this, he was bayoneted again and fell on his back. Lying on the ground, bleeding from his wounds, Vicente slurred to himself, "I'm sorry..." as he died.

40

B ara, in the forest, witnessed Juan's leap. The sight
of Juan falling made some Americans hesitate for a
moment. It gave the cadets time to reexamine their
thoughts. The leap gave the surviving cadets a boost to their
morale. The cadets didn't care if they lived or died. They all
had come to the same conclusion: fight to the death.

"Juan chose his destiny. Now we will choose ours. Will we
run, or will we fight?" Bara cried out.

"We will fight, sir!" The cadets answered in unison.

"This is our time—NOW! It has been my honor to command you all. Are you all with me?" Bara questioned to stir
the cadets. He saw their eyes, and they were not hesitating.

"We are with you, sir!" all the cadets yelled together.

Juan then pulled out his sword from its scabbard.

"Then death to our enemies who invade our beloved Mexico.
Show them death comes to us all and that we are not afraid of
it. Who wants to live forever, men?" Bara yelled proudly.

In a blink of an eye, the remaining cadets rose from the
trenches toward the overwhelming American army. As they

charged, the Americans yelled an order of surrender to the cadets. The cadets were still advancing. At first, the Americans thought the cadets didn't understand, but then they realized that they were all prepared to fight to the death. The cadets began firing at the soldiers with whatever was left of their ammunition, and the Americans fired back.

"*Por la patrriaaaa!*" Bara yelled with tears in his eyes.

The Americans fired their rifles. All that was left was a cloud of smoke. An eerie silence fell on the forest of Chapultepec. Through the smoke, only a handful of cadets still advanced toward the American army, including Agustin and Bara. Bara was shot in the arm, but it did not slow him down. They were able to engage the enemy, fighting hand to hand. A soldier shot Bara in the leg. Bara tried to get up but was shot again and fell to the ground bleeding. Bara died quickly, but Agustin continued to engage the Americans. He was outnumbered and was stabbed from behind. Agustin fell to the ground in agonizing pain. He couldn't get up. He twisted in agony at first, but then, suddenly, he stopped.

"I can smell the roses too, Merced. I smell them too..." Agustin said sadly, as he knew death was not far behind. He pictured his true love with one last smile as death embraced him.

After all the cadets in the forest were killed, many of the Americans stood still and bowed their heads in silence. Some soldiers crossed their chests with their hands in the sign of the cross. Others were finally realizing that these Mexican soldiers were nothing more than children, even younger than they were. The Americans were puzzled as to why children had been sent into battle.

41

Francisco Marquez was one of the few remaining cadets. Instead of fleeing, Francisco ran toward where Juan Escutia had fallen. Francisco dodged bullets and cannonballs. None of that mattered when he witnessed his roommate leap to his death. Francisco knew Juan was dead, but something inside him wanted to see Juan one last time. As he got closer, he found Juan lying on a large rock. Francisco needed to see if there was a chance that Juan had any signs of life. He continued to run rapidly, avoiding the bullets that were flying over his head. He was almost there. Francisco was surprised to see little a movement from Juan as he leaped toward him, trying to avoid stray projectiles. Francisco crawled over to Juan and hovered over him.

"Juan, can you hear me? Juan?" Francisco pleaded.

"Francisco, I can't see," Juan replied weakly.

"I'm here. It's all right," a relieved Francisco answered.

"You dumb fool, get out of here. Flee, now!" Juan said as blood flowed out of his mouth.

"Like you said before, we live together, we fight together," Francisco said as tears ran down his face.

"If you don't get out of here, we will die together. Get out of here now! Run!" Juan begged, struggling to talk.

"Let me give you your last rites," Francisco said as he started to compose himself.

"I'm fine with God now. We are settled," Juan said, and the pain grew as he talked.

"Well then, just answer me one thing before I go."

"Damn it, just go. Please, please, you have to live."

Francisco ignored Juan's plea. He continued to ask his question. "Were we ever friends?" Francisco muttered his words.

Realizing the question, Juan repeated Francisco's last word. "Friends?" Juan said. "Friends?" Juan said again, puzzled. He paused and with a slight smile answered Francisco with a smirk. "No."

Francisco was saddened by the answer and hung his head in embarrassment. Juan's smile slowly faded as he tried with all his might to lift his arm toward Francisco. Juan laid his hand on Francisco's shirt. Tears started to run down Juan's face, and, with his last ounce of strength, he tugged Francisco's shirt toward him, to whisper his final words into Francisco's ear. And with his final breath, Juan said, "We were more than that. We were brothers…"

Francisco could not believe his ears. With tears in his eyes, Francisco smiled, realizing they shared more than any other cadets at the academy.

"But I always thought, don't worry; I have my father's cross. I will say a small prayer for you before I go," Francisco said to himself in desperation. He searched for the cross around his neck, but it was not there. Frantically, he began looking for it. He spotted it on the ground a few feet away. It must have fallen off when he leaped to Juan. He started to reach for it but was immediately shot in the chest.

Francisco was on the ground full of pain, but he was not giving up. He was only a few feet away from his cross, and he reached for it. With tears in his eyes, he crawled in pain, knowing that if he could just grab his cross, he would feel the peace his mother had always told him about. He was so close now. He was stretching for the cross, digging his fingers and nails into the ground. The pain was unbearable. Francisco was only a foot away from his cross. He made one last attempt to reach for the cross, but an American sharpshooter took aim and killed him. Francisco died only a few inches away from his cross.

42

Colonel Clifford was assessing the aftermath. Many of his fellow soldiers were now rummaging through the dead cadets, trying to find anything they could salvage. Clifford hiked near the steep rocks where Juan Escutia and Francisco lay. He observed two American soldiers about to go through the pockets of the dead cadets. As they looked through their uniforms, Colonel Clifford got close enough to hear them talk.

"William, look what I found. A pen."

"That's nothing; I see a cross in the dirt. I think it's his by the way he wanted to clench it."

"Ya think its gold?"

As the soldier was about to pick it up, Colonel Clifford intervened. "Don't even think about it," Clifford said despairingly as he pulled out his pistol and pointed it toward the ground.

"But Colonel, it's the spoils of war," the soldier responded nervously. The two men started to reach for the cross cautiously.

"I won't say it again," Clifford said in a threatening tone. He cocked his pistol as he aimed it at the soldiers.

"Fine, Colonel, it's all yours. Let's get out of here. There are more dead Mexicans in the castle, anyway."

The two soldiers scurried away. Clifford walked over to the two dead bodies and saw Francisco's cross on the ground. He saw the faces of the dead cadets and imagined his sons before him. The whole ordeal was too much for him.

"But they were just children!" Colonel Clifford exclaimed, overwhelmed by emotion. In need of some kind of comfort, Clifford realized he still had his son's drawing. He reached inside his coat and took the picture out. He smiled as he saw a cartoonish picture of his family. Clifford began to fold it back up carefully, but then he noticed there was something written on the back. As he turned it around and unfolded it, he began to read his child's writing.

"I am so proud of you, Pa. I pray to God I can be as kind and as just as you someday."

As soon as Clifford finished reading his son's inscription, he fell to his knees and picked up Francisco's cross.

"I am so sorry," Clifford whispered.

As Clifford wept, he touched the dead cadet's hand and very gently laid Francisco's cross back into his hands. "Rest in peace, son. Rest in peace," Clifford said quietly as he continued to weep over the bodies.

43

Reverence

Back in Mexico City in March of 1947, a hundred years had passed since the battle of Chapultepec. A distinguished gentleman stood before the monument honoring the Niños heroes. The gentleman placed a wreath on the ground and bowed his head for a couple of minutes. There was a group of young cadets to his left who were students of a nearby military academy. They too were giving a morning tribute to the Niños heroes. While the cadets stood at attention, they saw the gentleman. Tears started to stream down their young faces as they watched his reverence. As the gentleman raised his head, he turned around to make his way back to his motorcade, escorted by many diplomats. Walking back, he broke away from the Secret Service to shake the hands of the Mexican people. When he finished, he was about to get into his vehicle, but several reporters rushed in and began asking him questions.

"Mr. Truman, sir."

"Mr. President, Mr. President."

He stopped and turned to them. "Yes?" he simply replied.

A hush came over the crowd. They were shocked that the president of the United States would stop so abruptly and answer their questions.

"Mr. President, why did you visit the monument this morning?"

With a sense of pride, the president answered, "Brave men don't belong to any one country. I respect bravery wherever I see it."

This answer left the reporters speechless. They stopped asking questions as they realized there was nothing left to ask. The president stepped back into his vehicle and left.

A light breeze glided over the trees in the forest nearby. A small, solid figure could be seen on the walkway at the top of Chapultepec Castle. The figure was a statue dedicated to one of the boy heroes. It was remarkably accurate to Juan Escutia's facial features. A small inscription at the bottom of the statue read, "Mexico's True Son."

The statue stood tall and proud, as though Juan's spirit would continue to oversee his beloved Mexico. For Mexico was a land worth fighting and dying for. The sun glistened over the statue as if God himself had blessed Juan Escutia's selfless act. The sun became so bright it faded everything to white.

Fin

EPILOGUE

The war was officially over in 1848. Nicholas Trist, President Polk's representative, was in Mexico City beginning discussions for a peace treaty with Mexican officials. Once the Treaty of Guadalupe had been signed, the news reached President Polk, who was satisfied with the outcome. Mexico ceded parts of Colorado, Arizona, New Mexico, Nevada, Utah, and Wyoming, as well as present-day California. Mexico received $15 million in compensation for war-related damages to Mexican property, half of what they had been offered before the war.

A month before the end of the war, Polk's actions were criticized in the US House of Representatives by General Zachary Taylor as "a war unnecessarily and unconstitutionally begun." Taylor, not happy with the administration, ran for president. Abraham Lincoln campaigned vigorously for Taylor, who became our twelfth president. General Winfield Scott ran for president in 1852 but lost. His opponent, Franklin Pierce, won what was considered to be one of the nation's largest electoral victories at that time, 254–42.

Fourteen years later, the United States went to war with itself. There were many reasons for this civil war. Many believed it was due to those who opposed the expansion of slavery into territories newly owned by the United States. When Ulysses S. Grant was asked about his reminiscences, he condemned the Mexican War, in which he had served, and even saw the Civil War as some sort of karmic retribution for America's sins against its southern neighbor.

ABOUT THE AUTHOR

E. Richard Amiel is the son of a Guatemalan father and Mexican mother and boasts a diverse background. He was born in East Los Angeles, where he has deep roots to the city. He has moved to several parts of the United States, but spent his teen years in Mexico. That is where he developed a fascination with the story of the forgotten young men who defended their country during the Mexican-American War.

A county worker for the city of Los Angeles by profession, Amiel prides himself on his acceptance and respect for all cultures, which he encounters on a daily basis. He has been researching these brave young men for the past ten years. He truly hopes that readers, young and old, will appreciate the sacrifice and valor Los Ninos Heroes gave for their country.

www.ingramcontent.com/pod-product-compliance
Lightning Source LLC
Chambersburg PA
CBHW061216170626
46809CB00003B/1375